Thicker Than Blood

By Bella Danielle Evans

Chapter 1

Sherri

The phone rang continuously and seemed to get louder. Warm sand between my toes and the cool, soothing ripples of the ocean kept me in a trance. The breeze caressed the loose flowing curls hanging from my head and I didn't want to move. The incessant ringing interrupted my slumber and reminded me that I was no longer on vacation but needed to address the crisis of the day at home. I rubbed my hand over my forehead in a failed attempt to suppress the headache that was rapidly forming. I glanced at the alarm clock next to me that read 8:52 am. Despite the protests of my heavy eyes and unwilling legs, I dragged myself to the edge of the bed and made my way into the shower. The cold water tap dancing on my face was just what I needed in order to operate on three hours of sleep. As I rubbed the sponge over my chocolate skin I remembered how Tyler's complexion matched mines. I imagined his big brown eyes and strong features that always seemed to make me feel secure. I needed to hear his voice. I needed him to help me relax before I exploded my unfortunate situation into a bigger mess than it needed to be. The phone rang again jolting me back to reality. I shut off the shower, grabbed my plush towel and raced to the front of my apartment to answer it. Before I could say hello the caller bombarded my eardrum.

"Well, it's about time you answered" my mom ranted. "I was starting to worry. I told you to call me as soon as your flight landed."

"I know ma, I'm sorry. I was so tired that I…"

"That's no excuse" she interrupted. "I didn't know if your plane crashed or you got kidnapped at the airport. You should have called."

"I know, I know. Now you know I'm fine. Do you want to have lunch?" I reluctantly offered.

"I'll be ready at 11:30."

I put the receiver back on the base and checked the caller ID to see if I missed any of Tyler's calls. Tyler and I have known each other since we were kids. We lived across the street from one another in a developing neighborhood in Greensboro, North Carolina. Tyler was like a brother to me, but that all changed once we started college at Winston Salem State. It was there that I met my "sisters." It has been a year since I graduated and we still remain close.

The only messages on the answering machine were from the landlord demanding the rent and Tammy trying to get everyone together for dinner this weekend. I picked up the phone to see if Kina was going but there wasn't a dial tone.

"Hello…" I said, checking if someone was on the line.

"Hi, I didn't hear the phone ring," Tyler answered.

"I was just about to make a call."

"Oh, should I call back later?" he quickly responded.

"No, I'm glad you called. I haven't talked to you since I left."

"I know; between night classes and your vacation" he paused "Anyway, I wanted to let you know that I'm moving closer to campus."

"Yeah, your mom mentioned it before I left. Why didn't you tell me yourself?" I asked revealing my frustration with his approach.

"It never seemed like the right time. Besides, I didn't want to put a damper on your trip."

"Why would that affect my trip? I figured you would move soon anyway." I waited for him to respond, "Is everything okay?"

"Yeah, everything's fine… but"

"But what?" I asked, pressing my ear to the phone, eager to hear his next words.

"I just think we need to slow things down a bit."

"Okay, what is that supposed to mean; we don't see each other as it is."

"I'm not breaking things off; I just think that we need to pause and reflect on our relationship and how things have changed. Besides you're practically out here every weekend visiting your friends anyway."

I took a moment to absorb what he said. He was right; the move in itself wasn't serious but something still nagged the innermost part of me like a silent warning.

"Are you still there?" he asked.

"Yes, I'm here…So when do you leave?"

"Actually, I'll be settled in by the end of the week. My dad's friend has a condo that he's letting me rent."

"Wow. I guess I will catch you before you leave."

"Yeah, I need to get ready for my shift at the hospital. Talk to you later."

I hung up the phone and drifted back into my room and sat on my unmade bed. I've always been able to tell what Tyler is thinking and predict his next move before he knew. Now I'm not so sure. With this unnecessary tension between me and Alexis brewing I couldn't stand to lose one of the strongest fighters in my corner. I brushed aside my feelings of doubt and got dressed. I needed to clear things up with my landlord before I was out on the street.

I tossed on a t-shirt and sweatpants and walked over to the rental office. As I got closer I felt my stomach knot up and my nerves went into overdrive. I paused for a moment in the parking lot to clear my head and try to go in calmly. I have been a great tenant and Ms. Bakulas was being unreasonable to demand the money the way she did, but I didn't want to blow up. As I was starting to relax Ms. Bakulas popped her head out the door and my muscles again tightened.

"The office is open," she called out, no doubt wondering why I was pacing in the parking lot. Her eyes almost seemed beady beneath her thick rimmed glasses. She is always a contrast of high energy bottled up in a tiny, frail body. Through the window I could see her quickly wobble back over to her desk and rummage through some files. I took a deep breath and entered the small office with a tight smile.

"Have a seat darling; I'm so glad to see you," she offered in the sweetest tone; such a contrast from the many messages I filtered through while I should have been relaxing at the beach. The law firm that I'm working with was taking part in a conference at Myrtle beach and I was being paid to be on vacation. The only thing missing was my girls but it was a business trip after all.

"Hmm, well I'm here," I replied standing in front of her gently placing the money order on the desk. I wanted this visit to be as short as possible so I declined the seat. Her brown and black, bobtail cat brushed pass my leg.

"I'm so sorry about your trip, but you understand," she mentioned as I was just turning to leave.

"Actually, I don't," I responded stopping to turn back to face her. "I have always paid my rent on time and I've never caused any problems or cause for concern. I assured you that this was something that I could have handled when I arrived next week. I don't understand why this could not have waited. After all you already had my half of the rent," I vented.

Her face was one of utter disbelief and I regretted my tone but not what I said.

"I cannot deposit assurances," she snapped. "Too many times I've seen you young people try and slide by a month and next thing you know you short me each month. You are a great tenant but the rent is the rent, and it's due the same time each month."

"You know," I stopped short recognizing where this conversation could go, "you have your rent. Have a good day." I turned to leave resisting all urge to slam the door.

Kina

I dismissed another e-mail from the editor of the Winston Salem Journal rushing an article that I was working on. My eyes were glued to an on-line blog revealing ten secrets to losing weight when I heard a knock at the door to my office. I quickly closed the screen and turned my attention to the door. Alexis walked in and shut the door behind her. Her hair hung to her shoulders with the natural wave that I envied. She was still dressed up from the interview she had with my superiors, her desirable curves minimized but still noticeable beneath her sophisticated outfit.
"Well, come on in," I joked as she took a seat across from my desk.
"Hey girl," she replied with a long face.
"What's going on?" I asked as I closed my laptop.
"I didn't get the internship I applied for."
"I'm sorry, I thought…"
"I got an internship with freelance opportunities," she interrupted, trying to contain her excitement. "It's not much but depending on my performance I might be able to get a permanent position. Thanks so much, girl, for putting in a word for me."
"Congrats, that was all you. My recommendation was just icing on the cake."

"I'm so excited. Let's go out and celebrate."

"I wish I could, but Micah and I are going out to dinner tonight. We can celebrate tomorrow, Sherri called me earlier and we are supposed to get up."

"I have to work at the store tomorrow."

"Have you spoken with Sherri since she got back?" I prodded sensing her reluctance to a group dinner.

"Briefly."

"Is she still mad about you ruining her trip," I jokingly asked to address the elephant in the room.

"Why you have to say it like that? I didn't ruin anything. I apologized for her having to come home a day early to take care of my half of the rent but I explained everything that is going on," she replied her voice stress getting higher.

"Okay; get out of your feelings! I was just making sure; you know how she can be."

"Yeah, and she knows how I am," she replied standing and flipping her hair over her shoulder. "I wouldn't have missed my share if it wasn't an emergency and I didn't honestly think Ms. Bakulas was going to trip like that."

I thought about telling her that it's no surprise that her realtor would want her money but I knew Lexie and she was coming from a good place.

"I'm just glad everything worked out," I said as I stood from the chair. I put away the papers scattered on my desk. "Well, I'm leaving early today. I'll call you later."

"Okay, thanks again. Tell Micah I said hi," she added before slipping out of the door.

The time seemed to drag as I sped down Franklin Avenue on the way to my condo. My dashboard blinked to remind me that I was at a quarter of a tank, but I didn't stop until I reached the parking space marked 302 in front of my home. My neighbor, Teresa, waved at me as I rushed up the sidewalk and I offered a quick nod signaling that I had no time to talk. I didn't want to get caught in conversation with her. She is always trying to get together with us but something seems off with her. I stepped out of my shoes in the foyer as I entered and hung my coat in the closet. After dialing Micah's number, I dropped my laptop on the sofa in the living room and headed to my room. I left a message on the voicemail confirming that we were supposed to meet at 7:30 and hopped into the shower. Micah and I met at a concert six weeks ago that Alexis and I attended. I was reluctant to open up to his smooth lines and charming smile but things have been going great so far. I hopped out of the shower and made my way to the bed where several outfits were thrown across it. I inspected and rejected each piece and settled on a black and turquoise kimono sleeve dress hanging in the closet. I was already self-conscious about the few pounds I put on and this dress was perfect at hiding it. I hung it on the hanger on the bedroom door and put on my coconut lime body lotion and spray. A quick glance at the alarm clock on my dresser revealed I was running late so I rushed to put my hair in a quick up-do and slid on the dress and matching earrings. By the time I was satisfied with the finished product my cell phone rang. I assumed it was Micah so I took a moment to pause so I wouldn't sound anxious as I answered.

"Hey babe," Micah spoke through phone.

"Hey, I just got dressed. Are you on your way?"

"No, I'm sorry. I'm not going to be able to make it tonight."

"Why not?" I asked flopping back on the bed.

"Fred called, he has another house to do tonight, so he asked if I could help. I hope you aren't mad."

"Hmm."

"I'm sorry. I know you looking cute for me too."

"Why don't you find out," I replied as slid off my heels realizing it was a lost cause.

"I would if I could. But I promise to make it up to you."

"You better," I retorted before hanging up.

I exhaled in frustration as I stood to change out of my dress. I contemplated his excuse for standing me up. His cousin Fred owns a private company that paints, restores, and repairs homes but I'm curious if that's truly what he is up to tonight. Alexis warned me to be cautious but at the same time I don't want to be suspicious or pushy. Past relationships and my own insecurities have left me damaged emotionally and my current weight battle is not helping. I thought about calling Alexis to see if she still wanted to go out. We decided to stay in so I slipped into some jeans and a t-shirt. I called in hibachi chicken and vegetables at our favorite Japanese restaurant and Alexis walked in with it shortly after. She had changed into some more casual clothes.

We both reclined on my sofa with our feet resting on the table next to our half empty trays of food and our stomachs full. I am an only child, so I cherished moments like these when we get together. I have grown to love all the girls in our circle but I have always felt more connected to Alexis. It's not something that I would repeat; I haven't even admitted out loud to Alexis, but we both know.

"Have you and Sherri made nice yet?" I asked.

"You could say that," she responded.

Alexis needed to move closer to her mom since her health was declining. She had a place lined up but there was another potential tenant trying to get the same apartment so Alexis had to close the deal before he gave the place away. I gave her a look saying that I know she could try more.

"Seriously, I apologized and told her I would pay her back as soon as I get my next check."

"So, I'll see you at dinner tomorrow?"

"No, I have to work."

"Okay, but we all have to get together soon."

"Yeah, I know. I've been so busy at the store and finishing up this last semester. And now, all this stuff with my mom…"

"Just let me know if I can help any."

Tammy

My heart was racing. A biker had just jetted off the curb right in the path of my new model sedan. I would have hated to mess up my Sonata but, truthfully, I was more concerned about hitting him; my conscience couldn't carry the guilt. My nerves were already on edge since I was in a rush to pick up my seven year old son, Roderick, from school. My managers do not care that I have children. While I was waiting at a light, I turned on the radio to calm my nerves. Between the sun beaming through the windshield and the heat blaring in the car, you wouldn't believe that it was 40 degrees outside. I turned the heat up some as I pulled into the circle in front of the elementary school. Rod was already outside waiting for me with his teacher, bundled up from head to toe with his toboggan, coat, and gloves. I waved at the two of them and his teacher gave a stiff nod and headed back inside without a word.
"I hope you weren't waiting long," I asked Rod as he entered the car.
"No, I just came outside. Mrs. Perry already graded my test; I only missed one spelling word."
"That's awesome! I knew you would do well."
"What's for dinner? I'm hungry."
"I don't know yet."

I called home to see if Janise, my ten-year-old daughter, had arrived home from school but there was no answer.

"So how was your day?" I asked him hoping to take my mind off the overwhelming list of things I had to do.

His big, brown eyes lit up with enthusiasm as he talked and he reminded me so much of his father. It wasn't long before we pulled into the paved driveway leading to our two story house. Janise was on the porch, talking on the phone which explained why she didn't pick up. Rod ran inside and put away his book bag and was back out before I finished gathering my things out of the car. I made my way up the lit, stone, walk way that led to the porch that was large enough for a swing and a rocker. My phone rang so I shuffled my bags to answer it and tripped on the first step of the porch. The stinging sensation running across my face reminded me of a pain I've felt too many times before. Looking at the concerned look on my children's faces, I remembered one of the horrifying experiences I had almost two years ago.

It was near the end of the summer and I was out shopping for the children's school clothes. I entered the house, about ten minutes later than expected, and was greeted by the stone hard fist of a 6 foot 3 inch, 215 pound man. Like a feather my 5 ft 3 inch frame fell to the floor, experience telling me to lay motionless.

"You were supposed to be home by 9! It don't take that long to get clothes. You trying to get with somebody else?" my husband yelled.

Pain from his kick surged up my side and into my chest limiting my response.

"No, I would never do that," I uttered.

"I know you were up to something hanging with them no good heifers," he insisted as he dragged me up the stairs into the bedroom, Hennessey seeping through his pores. "You telling them our business? Huh? They sitting around talking junk about me," then came a slap that made my ears ring. "I don't want you hanging with them no more," he demanded, "go wash yourself up before the kids wake up and see how stupid their mama is."

I rushed to the bathroom but not quick enough to miss the tear stained face of eight year old Janise. I closed the door to the bathroom, dreading what the mirror would reveal. With my eyes clouded with tears I cleaned my face as best as I could.

"Hurry up in there and get supper ready," his baritone voice rang. I opened my eyes to do a once over noticing how my once sparkling, almond shaped eyes were now dull and full of pain and regret. My once flawless skin now bruised. Janise's face etched in my mind I knew that this couldn't continue. On the way to the kitchen I comforted Janise and Roderick.

"Mommy is okay. Go get dressed and put on cartoons until the food gets ready."

"Yes ma'am," they solemnly replied in unison.

"What is taking so long," he yelled a half hour later as I was just about to plate the food.

"Dinner is ready," I replied nonchalantly.

"You talking back," he said in a voice so low it sent chills up my spine. As he rushed past the table towards me I heard someone at the door. Thankful for the interruption I rushed to answer it.

"Good morning… are you all right?" the well dressed woman asked pausing no doubt noticing my distressed state.

"Yes," I answered, "but I'm busy."

"Well, we won't keep you. I'd like to leave you this Bible based pamphlet which discusses why we suffer. Can I come back at a better time?"

Today, that scene is as fresh in my mind as if it happened yesterday and the look on my children's faces invoked that same sense of obligation to comfort them, "I'm okay, just little scrapes and bruises. Go ahead in and start your homework while I get dinner ready. Matter of fact, lets order in, how about pizza?"

"Yeah," they answered simultaneously.

I went inside and ordered the pizza and got cleaned up. I thought that the call that preceded my fall may have been Sherri calling about tomorrow's dinner but it was from my coworker Stephanie. She and her eight year old son, J.B., were coming over. Stephanie is also a single mom that works with me as a computer programmer. She had her son when she was young and his father hasn't been in their life since he signed the birth certificate. Stephanie's mom practically raised J.B while she went to college. I changed out of my work clothes and threw on some jeans and a t-shirt. By the time I finished straightening up Stephanie and J.B. were at my doorstep. Stephanie gracefully flowed in the house wearing her DKNY pantsuit and Christian Dior shades even though the sun was setting. I sent J.B. off to play with Rod so she and I could talk. I led her into the living room and she sat down on the cream sofa across from the T.V. Since it was growing dark outside, I walked over to close the drapes and turn on the floor lamp. I sat down next to Stephanie who had pushed her hair back with the sunglasses and looked at me, eyes wide. I grabbed the remote off the coffee table so that I could turn down the volume on the television.

"It seems like it's been months since we've gotten together outside work; how have you been?" I asked her.

"I've been doing great. I'm seeing this guy named Bradley and we have been hitting it off really well; J.B. loves him."

"He's not the only one; look at you, you are glowing," I teased.

"I know. He invited me and J.B. to move in with him since I've been struggling with the bills lately. I think I might take him up on his offer."

"Don't you think it's too soon?"

"I don't think so, he's a nice guy and he's really great with J.B. Plus, it will be good for him to have a male role model around."

"How long have you been dating?"

"Three months."

"And you are just now telling me," I said as I playfully tapped her arm.

"I didn't want to say anything because I didn't think it would be serious."

"Still, you tell me about every other fling that you have; I'm starting to think you were trying to hide him. Is he ugly or something?"

"Stop! You should know me better than that."

"I do, and I know you like to rush into things too soon."

"We have a great connection. The chemistry between us is… amazing."

"That's great but even serial killers are cunning enough to bring home a wife. You need to be sure about him before you talk about moving in with him since you have a son."

"I know things are moving quickly but J.B. and I both have spent a lot of time with him."

"Where did you meet him?"

"At Precision Tune when I was getting an oil change."

"You're dating your mechanic?"

"What's wrong with that?" She asked, pretending to be offended.

"Nothing; just don't show up to work with any grease stains."

Alexis

"Hey girl, you ready to go," Missy called from the back. We were just finishing up a day of work at Glam, a local fashion store.
"Yeah, just let me get my things together."
"So, what you think about the job so far?" she asked as she came to the counter wearing something I wouldn't be caught dead in. She wore a dress with a v-neck too far down her chest and just barely covered her thick hips. With her four inch heels that wrapped around her legs she was almost as tall as I am.
"It pays the bills" I replied while mustering up a smile.
"It gets better," she assured me as she locked the door to the store and set the alarm. "Bridgette comes through sometimes and she is always looking for new people to model at the annual show in New York. One girl got promoted and got hired at the New York office full time."
"When I move to New York it will be because of my writing. But I can't move right now anyway," I responded.
"I don't want to move my kids either."
"I didn't know you had children" I replied as I followed her to her car. She was driving a 2009 Nissan Maxima and it had baby seats and empty juice boxes in the back.

"I have two. Miguel is 5 and Miyah turned 4 a couple weeks ago," she added with no hint of enthusiasm. "So did you get the internship at the Winston Salem Journal?" she asked quickly changing the subject.

"Yeah, I'll be working on-line with Kina. Hopefully I'll be able to write my own articles soon."

"Have you met the night manager here, Jerry?" she asked, again shifting topics.

"Not yet, why?"

"Well he's noticed you. He was asking about you today. Girl, I think he was checking you out."

"I hope not, because I'm not interested," I replied as I fastened my seatbelt signaling that I was ready to go.

"Why not? Girl he is fine and he has money. If I didn't have two kids and a crazy baby daddy I would be on that myself."

"Wow you are too much," I said jokingly but meant every word.

"Where do you want to eat because I'm starving?" I asked reminding her that we actually had somewhere to be. I don't usually hang out with my co-workers but I found out that Missy is my cousin on my Dad's side of the family. She grew up in D.C. around my brother Alex or Lex as we call him.

"Let's go to Mi Casa," she suggested and finally exited the parking lot.

"That's cool."

"What made you move to the 'tre four'?" she asked referring to Winston-Salem.

"Well Kina told me about the internship plus I wanted to be closer to my mom since she's been sick."

"That's right; Lex was telling me about that. Is she doing okay?"

"She's doing pretty well. She just can't get around like she used to," I answered remembering that I needed to stop by and see her. She scared us when she had an asthma attack and ended up in the hospital because she was alone without her inhaler. With Lex working harder to take care of his developing family he can't be with her as much as we would like.

"Have you met Lex's baby-mama, Trina, yet?" Missy asked breaking the silence.

"No, I'm going over there tomorrow. Have you?"

"I've met her a couple of times. She's a lyricist that has been working with Lex but I don't know too much about her. She's a little ghetto though."

"Really," I said wondering how she had room to talk.

"Anyway, I'm glad we got a chance to get together. Big Al and Lex used to talk about you all the time."

"Is that right," I asked surprised at the news. Lex called me almost every day but my dad, Big Al, rarely asked for me to visit him after my mom left him when I was 9. My mom never gave me a reason for her leaving. All I remember is coming home from school one day and all of our things were packed. My mom was crying and she told me to get in the car no questions asked. After about an hour's drive she finally told me we were going to my Aunt Meghan's house and that Lex wasn't coming with us. I blamed my mom for a long time for breaking up our family and even accused her of keeping my father from me.

"Yeah. Sometimes it was if you were growing up with us. I used to call you my imaginary cousin. I can only remember you visiting once."

"Yeah, I didn't get up there much," I replied with a sigh. "Lex usually came to see us here instead," I added.

"I guess the 'family business' was not a place for a young girl to be around."

"Right," I offered. I knew the gist of my family's past but I wondered if she would be willing to reveal more than my mom or brother.

"But the past is the past right," she went on.

"So, are you still with Miyah and Miguel's father," I asked sensing that I shouldn't push for more information yet.

"Please!" she responded as if it was an outlandish idea, "don't get me started on them. Miguel's dad split after the first year and Miyah's father is in prison. I'm holding him down in spirit but on the outside a girl gotta do what she can to get by, you know what I mean."

I nodded in affirmation wondering what all she was doing to get by.

Tammy

Before I left work I called Kenny's mother, Mama Rose, to see if she could watch Janise and Rod while I went out to dinner with the girls. She picked them up after school and they were still at her place. She agreed and asked to watch them for the night. Not long after I hung up Stephanie came by my office to catch me before I left.

"Hey girl; what you doing tonight?" she asked.

"I'm going out to eat with Sherri and Kina; you wanna come?"

"Actually, I'm going out with Bradley. I was hoping J.B. and Rod could hang out but I guess I'll call my mom to see if she'll watch him."

"Where are y'all going?"

"He's taking me to this comedy club called Funny Bone; Ricky Smiley is supposed to be performing there."

"Oh yeah, I heard about that," I mentioned as I logged of the computer and grabbed my purse.

"Did I tell you that I'm moving in with him at the end of the month when my lease is up?" she added before we exited the office.

"You told me you were thinking about it; I didn't know you made it definite."

"Yep, check out the ring," she said showing me her modestly cut diamond ring.

"Congratulations! I'm happy for you but are you sure you're ready; y'all just met a couple of months ago."

"I know he's the one; I'm so excited."

"I want you to be happy but…."

"Thank you for supporting me girl," she said hugging me before I could state my objection.

"Well, I have to go drop some clothes off for the kids and get ready, let's get together tomorrow," I said as I exited the building. It was only thirty minutes until I was supposed to be at Sherri's apartment and I still had to drop some clothes and snacks off at Mama Rose's.

"Hey sweetie," she greeted me at the door. Mama Rose must have a week's worth of house robes because every time I see her she has a different one on. Her hair is always in rollers and she had her house slippers on.

"Hey. Thanks again for watching the kids."

"Honey please, it's not baby-sitting when it's your grandchildren. Besides I want as much time with them as I can get in my old age."

"I'm sure you have plenty more to go," I assured before turning to go.

"Let me ask you something before you leave," she added.

"Of course," I responded though I was more than late.

"You know Kenny is really trying this time and the year he spent in prison…"

"Mama Rose," I interjected.

"I know my son isn't perfect," she interrupted, "and I don't agree with what he did to you. But he loves you and he wants to do right by his family."

"I thought you wanted to ask me something," I reminded her hoping she would get to the point soon.

"Will you at least talk to him?"

"We'll see," I offered knowing that I had no intention of talking to him. One thing I learned the hard way is that his promises are easily broken. "I really have to go."

"Mmm hmm," she replied knowing that I wouldn't. "Enjoy your evening."

Finally, I arrived at Oak Crest Lane and pulled in the parking lot to Sherri's complex.

"It's about time you got here," Sherri called as I walked in the door to her apartment. Sounds of jazz welcomed me as I brushed past the coat hanger by the door and made my way into the living room where they were waiting. Kina and Sherri were sitting on the leather couch facing the blank television. Sherri had make-up on and a nice fitting dress. She has gained several pounds since we met freshman year but she carries it well. Kina looked great as usual. I always told her that she should have gone into television instead of writing.

"I was just about to put out an APB," Kina said as she stood up to give me a hug, "How are you? I can't believe you are kid free tonight."

"I'm good, and the kids are with their grandma. Don't you look cute?" I replied as I admired the outfit Kina was wearing.

"I try," she said as she did a spin showing off how her jeans hugged her hips just right and her top that showed off her waist line. "Y'all decided where we're going to eat?" she asked.

"Not yet, I was thinking about going to Mi Casa again but I hate to go to Winston for it," Sherri replied.

"Well," Kina said, "that sounds good to me; the food is great and their margaritas are even better."

"I'm in," I added.

"Okay... what about after that?" Kina asked.

Sherri chimed in, "well nothing is set in stone. I have games and cards we can play...I also have that new Tyler Perry movie...or we can go out to that Jazz club, the Renaissance."

"That sounds good," I said, "It'll give us a chance to relax."

"Yeah," Kina agreed, "and dance," then she did an imitation of the stankky legg and we all laughed.

"Okay.," Sherri replied, "let's get a move on before the place gets too crowded. Y'all can ride with me."

"When was the last time you spoke to Alexis," I asked Sherri.

"I talked to her yesterday. She came with her brother to pick up some things."

"So, what's up with you and Micah," Sherri asked as she popped in the new Chrisette Michele album into the CD player of her Kia Sportage.

"Girl I don't know. I think he's seeing somebody else. I haven't caught him in anything but I just know," Kina replied.

"Have you said anything to him about it?" I asked.

"No because it's never anything I can prove…but if he's doing something he'll slip up eventually."

"They all do. You could call that show Cheaters," Sherri joked.

"Right. But it's not even worth all that. We just started talking and if I can't trust him already then there's no need for us to keep seeing each other."

"I feel you," Sherri answered.

We finally arrived to the restaurant and the place was crowded.

"We aren't the only ones living 'la vida loca' tonight," Kina joked.

"I don't know why she would even consider leaving the house like that," I said noticing a woman sitting a couple of tables over from where we were standing. She had on a dress that was way too revealing for this type of restaurant and the weather.

"Wait a minute, isn't that Alexis?" Sherri asked.

"Not dressed like that," Kina said in disagreement.

"No, at the table with her."

"Yeah, that's her. I wonder who that is she's with," I said then waved as she looked our way, "here she comes."

"Hey ladies," she said as she approached us.

"I see you finally got off of work," Sherri teased.

"I called the house earlier…," Alexis replied.

"Yeah, I got your message. I called back but I didn't get an answer," Sherri responded and for a moment everyone could notice some tension lingering.

"So… who are you here with," I asked Alexis, curiosity getting the best of me.

"Oh, that's my cousin Missy."

"I don't think we've met. You two should join us," Kina mentioned.

"That's because we just met," Alexis replied, "We are actually just finishing dinner. Next time though."

"Isaiah called for you," Sherri blurted to Alexis before she could walk off. "He didn't have your cell number; I wasn't sure if I should give it to him."

"Nah; I'll call him later. Did I get any mail?" Alexis asked.

"Yeah," Sherri answered, "you have a couple of things at the house."

"Okay, I'll drop by later to pick it up."

"That was interesting," I said as Alexis was walking away. Before anyone could respond our host came over to seat us.

"Buenas noches, I'm Carlos. Table for 3?"

"Four," Kina responded and we both turned to her in confusion. "I was hoping you could join us."

"If only I could, senorita. Right this way, ladies," he said as he led us to our table. "Froy is going to be taking care of you tonight…"

"Aww, I was just getting used to you," Kina flirted.

"Okay," Sherri interrupted, "Thank you Carlos."

"No problema, maybe I'll check back in on you ladies later to make sure Froy gives you the best service," he said looking at Kina.

"I'm looking forward to it," she responded.

"I thought you were still going out with Micah," I asked Kina as Carlos walked away.

"Yeah I am. That doesn't mean I can't still test the waters. I don't have a ring yet."

"Look at you, and you had the nerve to be talking about Micah. You know the suspicious people are usually the guilty ones." Sherri suggested.

"Whatever, I haven't done anything. Besides if Micah is guilty of something I want to leave my options open."

"With the waiter?" I asked sarcastically

"First of all," Kina replied jokingly, making a list with her fingers, "he's our host. And B, I was just having fun. A little flirting doesn't do anything but boost your ego."

"B...?" I asked laughing at her mix-up.

"Maybe you should lay off the margaritas tonight because you are already crazy," Sherri replied shaking her head. Froy walked over to take our drink orders.

"I thought Alexis couldn't come because she had to work," Sherri asked after he left the table, "I guess she meant she couldn't come with us."

"She did have to work," Kina defended, "they probably stopped here after."

"I'm sure it was innocent," I added.

"Tammy, how is everything going with your divorce?" Sherri asked me after letting the thought marinate.

"Kenny refuses to sign the papers so it's dragging the process along."

"That is ridiculous," Sherri said, "the least he could do is sign the papers after all he put you through. He needs to get a life and stop stressing yours."

"Well, if he is a problem, I know somebody, that knows somebody, that robbed somebody that can take care of him," Kina said convincingly and then we all burst into laughter.

"Well after a few more drinks and a couple more of his drive by's I might consider it."

"Girl, no he is not driving by your house," Kina said a little too loudly.

"I seen his car once for sure but I may just be a little paranoid."

"You might need to get a restraining order," Sherri suggested.

"I thought about it, but I know he's just trying to catch me with some guy and I'm not worrying about that."

"Well, you be careful," Kina said, "and get you some mace, a dog, or something."

"Or I'll call the person you know," I joked.

Chapter 2

Alexis

I kept replaying my dinner with my cousin in my head as I headed to Sherri's apartment. I couldn't believe the negative attention Missy drew at the restaurant. She is family but we come from two different worlds. Still there was a weird connection between the two of us. I almost envy the time she had with my father and brother in D.C. Being with her is almost like filling in the gaps of what my brother is unwilling or unable to talk about. As I headed to Sherri's apartment to get my mail I wondered what she would have to say about our encounter last night. Luckily she wasn't at home. I found the mail on the table by the door. One of the letters didn't have a name of the sender. Inside there was a small note that read:

I want my money by the end of the week

I couldn't believe how Sherri was acting about any money after I explained everything that was going on. And she had the audacity to give me a deadline like she's some kind of loan shark. I don't know why she didn't say anything in person. I hurried and left before I she came home because I did not want to deal with her right now. Plus, I needed to buy a baby shower gift for my sister-in-law, Trina, before I started the first day of my internship at the Winston Salem Journal. In the car I called Isaiah to see what he wanted but I didn't get him on the phone. We went out on several dates but I couldn't connect with him like he claims he does with me. Missy asked to tag along when I told her I was getting Trina a gift, so I called her and told her to meet me at Baby's R Us. She came in with her daughter Miyah; thankfully she was dressed appropriately today wearing jeans and a t-shirt.

"What's up chick," she said as she got a buggy.

"Not much. You doing all right?"

"Always. Have you been by to see Trina yet?"

"Yeah, I went over last night." I answered.

"So, what you think about her?"

"A little extra, but she's cool," I replied walking towards the back of the store.

"So, you like her?"

"She's all right; why?"

"Well, that determines the gift we get," she said laughing at her own joke and I couldn't help laughing at her.

"She's okay," I answered, "I just want to get something they will definitely need for the baby."

"Cool. At least Lex is around to buy the stuff she needs unlike my tired babies daddies. I should've got me a man that was ballin' like your brother, then I wouldn't have to be struggling."

"Whatever, he does okay, besides, money isn't everything."

"You right, it aint. But it sure sell's the man for me right about now. Like this guy I met the other day, his chain distracted me long enough for me to give him my number."

We both burst into laughter.

"You are too much," I commented.

"Whatever, I got a car payment coming up. Besides, not everybody has the boss checking for them."

"What is that supposed to mean?"

"Girl, you know good and well what I'm talking about," she replied looking at me sideways.

"Not really, besides I'm not interested in him in that way."

"Please, you are so naïve. We'll see how long you last after them g's keep dropping in your account," she said, jealousy written across her forehead.

"I don't even see that happening, and if it did I wouldn't want it. Besides we are here for a gift," I said turning the corner of the crib aisle towards the baby clothes. Suddenly I regretted her being here.

"Are you seeing anybody, though?" she asked recognizing my frustration with her accusations about Jerry.

"Not really," I stated not wanting to get into my personal life to much until I found out more about Missy.

"What does that mean? That was a yes or no question" she asked her eyes fixed on me searching for some kind of leak.

"Well there is this guy I'm talking to, but I don't see us going anywhere," I finally offered.

"What's his name?"

"You wouldn't know him; I met him before I moved out here."

"At least you aint gay; I was a little worried for a minute," she replied finally letting the topic go.

"Wow, don't even go there," I said jokingly but starting to question if I could see myself actually opening up to Missy. It wasn't as if I was short on drama with my friends. I still needed to find out more about what went on in D.C. since my mom and my brother were so tight lipped about everything. If nothing else, Missy was the ticket to answering some unanswered questions about my past.

In the end, Missy slowed me down more than she helped me at the store. Eventually, I settled on a couple of outfits along with some baby products. Missy bought some outfits that she sent with me since I was heading to their house.

"Hey sis," Trina greeted me as I walked into their three bedroom home. The lights were low and I could barely see the all black living room now decorated with baby gifts and supplies.

"How are you feeling?" I asked following Trina to the sofa.

"I'm good. I'm so ready to drop this baby. I'm tired all the time and I can't get out the house like I used to. At least I've been able to write a lot of music."

"Well get used to it; you won't be able to hang once the baby gets here either."

"Girl bye, I'll strap her on my hip and keep it moving," she joked.

"Where's Lex?"

"At the studio. Matter of fact, can you take me down there? I need to lay a track and the doctor said I can't drive since I'm due any time now."

"No problem. Just don't go breaking your water in my car; I just had it detailed."

I was glad to take her since I hadn't been to Lex's studio yet. When my brother moved to Winston he went to a community college to get a degree in Entertainment Technology. He bought a studio with the money he got from selling the store after Dad died. It was bigger than I thought it would be; I expected a one room deal hooked on to a house or building or something. I actually never thought much of the music game other than copping an album from Target once in a while. But Lex is determined to be the next Swiss Beatz and I hope this angle will be successful enough to keep him out of trouble.

The studio was only a few miles from Lex and Trina's place. Kivette Drive veered to the left and I turned my Taurus to the right entering the small parking lot in front of the building where Lex made his living. He told me he sold songs to some famous musicians but looking at the modest structure you wouldn't imagine them being here. Trina instructed me to park in the space marked by a handicap sign and I reluctantly obliged after she assured me that I would be fine. I parked the car and Trina wobbled towards the door to have it opened for her by a large, muscular man who was obviously part of security. Just as I was wondering why such a humble space needed security, I walked into a nicely decorated lobby. To the left there was a room with glass doors and contemporary style furniture. There were a group of guys hanging in the lobby talking too loud to be in a place of business.

"Hey girl, come here," one of the men called out to me.

"Who is he talking to," I asked Trina annoyed.

"I'm talking to you," he replied heading our way. "Me and my boys are heading to Vivaldi's; why don't you ride with us?"

"No thank you," I stiffly answered.

"Girl, do you know who I am?" he asked extending his arms as if his status was significant.

"Killa Ka$h?" I retorted sarcastically.

"So you do know good music," he said seemingly satisfied with my response.

"No, I can read," I countered as I pointed to his name on his diamond laced chain that hung to his stomach.

"Okay, okay, you got sass; I like that. Well if you give me your number I could take you out on a proper date."

"I'm really not interested." I replied walking away from him towards Trina.

"It's like that?" he asked pretending to be offended.

"Just like that," Trina butted in, "I'm sure Lex won't appreciate you pushing up on his sister."

"My bad," he said throwing his hands up in defeat and headed back over to his entourage.

I followed her over to the desk where a young girl was manning the phones. She had on an American Eagle t-shirt and looked a little casual to be a receptionist.

"Hey Kelly," Trina greeted her.

"Aren't you supposed to be laid up in a bed somewhere?" she asked teasingly.

"I have been in the bed all day. Where's Lex?" she answered not pleased at her attempt at humor.

"I think he's in the control room. He just got finished working with Ka$h."

"Thanks" she said and we headed towards the elevator at the end of the hallway.

We exited on the second floor and entered the studio which had a hint of smoke in the air.

Lex was seated to the right with another gentleman in front of what I assumed to be the mixing station. There was also a sound proof recording room separated by a glass window. The recording area was dimly lit by a fluorescent light that almost inspired me to want to spit a few bars.

"Hey mama, what you doing here," Lex asked as he came over to hug Trina.

"I wanted to lay that track that I been working on."

"Hey Baby Sis, I'm surprised to see you here," he said hugging me as well.

"I'm not staying I just wanted to come in and speak. I hardly get to see you since you're working all the time."

"I know; I'm trying to get my money right before baby girl gets here."

"I hear ya," I replied.

"You can't speak," asked a man who looked as if he was in his mid-twenties but rough around the edges. Life has a way of draining the youth away from some folks. I hadn't' noticed him before; he was sitting next to the mixing station in front of a laptop.

"Hey," I responded then turned back to Lex."

"You remember J.O.," Lex reminded me.

"Oh, hey," I again greeted Lex's longtime friend and co-producer. He stood to give me a hug. "I haven't seen you in forever; you cut your hair," I added.

"You know, gotta keep it clean," he said smoothing his hand across his scalp.

"It was good seeing you again J.O.. I'm headed out; Lex, I'll see you Sunday at Mama's."

Kina

After another missed date with Micah, I decided to get some work done. Since I left my notes at the Journal, I threw on my sundress that covers my bulging belly and made a mental note to start going back to the gym. My high school years were horrible because of my weight and I refuse to get that big again. I got into shape by joining a hip hop class and stepping at WSSU. But since I graduated I have slacked on my exercise. I threw my hair in a ponytail and headed to the Journal. Another car pulled in beside me and I was relieved that it was only Alexis. I wasn't in the mood to deal with anyone from the office today.

"Hey girl, I thought you were going out with Micah," Alexis stated as she hopped out of her car.

"So did I," I replied upset that he stood me up again. "I don't know what to do with him. I don't want to seem like I'm stressing him but at the same time he's been a little suspect these past few weeks."

We started towards the tall white building beautifully decorated with blue glass windows.

"If you are interested in him you need to be up front with him now. Let him know that you need someone who is consistent, otherwise he will keep trying you."

"But he already says that I pressure him, I'd hate to push him away."

"If he is genuine that shouldn't bother him, and if it does than obviously he isn't looking for a commitment. And if that's what you're looking for then you should look for someone who will respect that."

"You're right," I conceded as we entered the elevator and I pushed the gold number four. "I'm tired of playing games with him, either he wants to be with me or he doesn't."

Alexis nodded her head in confirmation.

"What are you working on?" I asked.

"I did some research on a hair show that Michelle insisted that I attend."

"I thought you wanted to focus on investigative reporting and news?"

"I do, that's why I also researched the stomach virus that's going around. It's mostly affecting preteens and I think it has something to do with one of the schools. I also have some articles to proof read. You know exclusive stuff," she joked, "What are you working on?"

"I have to finish working on that article about the single parent support group that is misusing donations. Speaking of single people, you're done with Isaiah right?" I poked as we got off on our floor.

45

"Okay, that was a leap…Anyway I'm not sure. I hadn't heard from him since I moved and out of the blue he calls the apartment. I called back when Sherri gave me the message but I still didn't reach him."

"Well, I know someone that you should talk to," I brought up as we paused in front of the elevator.

"I don't think so."

"You should give him a chance, he's a good guy."

"If he's so great why don't you talk to him?"

"Because, I'm still sorting it through with Micah besides he asked about you."

"I know him?"

"His name is Eugene. He works here and he asked about your situation."

"Tell him I'm satisfied with my situation."

"I'm not asking you to marry the guy. You need a break from work and family."

"Yeah, but I remember the last guy you hooked me up with and I don't trust your judgment."

"Hey, you and Dennis were good together; you were the one who broke things off because you didn't feel like being in a relationship."

"No, I'm not talking about Dennis. I'm talking about the trainer who was either on the phone or in the mirror the entire dinner."

"I forgot about Phillip," I admitted, "but I didn't really know him."
"You knew he didn't have an inside voice; the whole time he sounded like the incredible hulk."
I couldn't help but laugh, "Yeah, he was bad. Anyway, that is water under the bridge. Eugene is cool."
"I appreciate it but," she paused as someone came over to get on the elevator. We started down the hallway toward her cubicle and she continued in a lower voice, "I'm not looking to kindle any office flame."
"All right," I conceded, "I'm going to head to my office and take care of this article. Check in with me before you leave maybe we can do something."
She agreed and I made my way pass the workspaces and to my office at the end of the hall. I contemplated what Alexis said about confronting Micah about his motives. After taking a seat at my cherry wood desk and starting up my laptop, I searched the drawers for the notes I had from my source in the single parent group. Once I had what I was looking for, I lost my desire to write. Questions about Micah's sincerity lingered in my mind and the reporter in me compelled me to take Alexis' advice and get to the bottom of it. I logged in on my laptop to appear working then picked up my phone to leave Micah a message since he was supposed to be helping his cousin finish a job.
After the third ring Micah answered the phone.

"Hey, I didn't expect you to answer," I confessed.

"Yeah, well, every call from my lady is important to me," he responded winning a cool point with me.

"Your lady huh," I asked probing his view of our relationship.

"Of course. At least that's what I thought this last month has led up to," he answered, the sound of buzzing and hammering in the background. Suddenly, I felt stupid for making the call.

"I'm glad to hear that I'm not in this alone," I opened up.

"Good, but surely that's not why you called."

"You're right," I came back quickly, now feeling as if I was on the hot seat. "I was just going to say that I hate that we couldn't get up and to call me when you were confident that you would show up." I was satisfied with the off the cuff remark. After all it was honest. He apologized again and we agreed to talk tomorrow. I hung up the phone hopeful of our relationship. Even though this was the second time in a row that he's stood me up I still felt optimistic.

I finally finished the article and called Sherri and Tammy to see if they wanted to get together with Alexis and I this evening. Even though Alexis said she and Sherri were cool I wanted to be sure that the two of them smoothed things out. My girls are the closest thing I have to family since my parents died. Tammy couldn't find a baby-sitter so she asked for us to come over her place. I found Alexis and told her about the plan for the evening.

"I guess we can make it a group thing," she reluctantly obliged.

"What's the big deal, I thought you and Sherri got over the rent thing."

"I thought we did too but she is acting funny over the rent. I didn't want to see her until I got my check."

"I'm sure she won't make that big a deal out of it," I replied hoping it was true.

We both took our cars and met at Tammy's. Sherri was already there. I met Alexis at her car and gave her a big smile hoping that all would go well tonight. She stretched her mouth into what would seem like a smile to someone who doesn't know her like I do.

"Hey everybody," I greeted as we entered and I took a seat on the couch next to Sherri. Alexis said her hello's as well. Tammy led us into her den. She had on a sundress that complimented her. You wouldn't guess she had two kids by looking at her. She was thick in the right places but to hear her tell it she is the biggest she ever been.

"Where's Janise and Rod," Alexis asked.

"Upstairs doing their homework. Y'all want anything to eat."

"Tammy threw down on her lasagna," Sherri complimented.

"Actually, Janise made it," Tammy corrected, "With supervision of course."

I declined the offer but Alexis went and made herself a plate then joined us in the love seat across from me and Sherri. Tammy sat in the armchair next to Alexis.

"So what's been going on," Tammy asked the group.

"Unfortunately nothing," I responded. The rest of the girls nodded their head in agreement. "Alexis, have you had any interesting assignments other than proofreading yet," I asked.

"Not really, and my food poisoning research was passed to another reporter. They want me to focus on more 'entertaining articles that will attract a younger audience.' I know this just an internship but I don't want to get stereotyped into this style of writing. I want to work on reporting current events and hopefully land the attention of an editor somewhere, you know."

"Just keep writing what you are interested in, who knows when your shot will come," I encouraged her.

"Do you have much time for writing since you've been taking care of your mom," Sherri asked, "I don't see how you find the time."

"I make time," she briefly answered and took a bite of her remaining food.

"That would explain why you don't have time for your friends anymore," Sherri retorted.

"I'm not even going to respond to that," Alexis returned.

"At least explain why you stood us up at dinner for someone you barely even know," Sherri pressed.

"I told you I had to work; leave it to you to make a big deal out of nothing."

Tammy and I looked at each other knowing where this conversation could go. Before either of us could change the subject Sherri continued the issue.

"Whatever, just remember who was there for you when you needed it."

"Where is all this coming from, really, because I know you aren't upset over a dinner," Alexis asked in frustration.

"You're right it's not just dinner. It's like you have been avoiding us lately. Or maybe just me."

"Of course, it's all about you," Alexis snapped.

"Like I said, you remember who had your back in college before you go burning bridges."

"What are you talking about?"

"Do you really have to ask?"

"Well, while you are running down memory lane, you keep in mind that I covered for you during your junior year too."

"Okay, let's not go there," Tammy intervened.

"Right, this conversation went from 1 to 10 in 3.5 seconds," I added, "We all have been busy and I don't think anyone has been able to make every 'get together.' Since college it's been rough for all of us."

"Exactly," Tammy continued, "so let's enjoy tonight. Alexis, do you have any graduation plans yet?"

Sherri went to the kitchen for a moment and Alexis settled back down in her chair. Alexis let out a breath and tried to make the best of the situation.

"Nothing yet," she finally answered. "Between mom being sick, my job and the internship, my hands are full. I doubt if I will do anything major."

Sherri finally joined us again and took her seat next to me. I nudged her and she gave an uneasy smile.

"We have to do something," Tammy objected, "don't you worry about it we will figure something out."

"Really, it's not that serious."

"It is too," I added. "Tammy's right, we will think of something, you just leave it to us."

Alexis gave in realizing that we wouldn't let it go, then took her plate back into the kitchen.

Sherri

One of the lawyers at the firm asked me to stay a few minutes late to finish reviewing a deposition and it turned into over an hour. As a paralegal I'm usually busy but the argument between Alexis and I replayed in my head and kept me from focusing on work. I couldn't believe she brought up what happened junior year. I'm glad it didn't go any further because Tammy and Kina do not know what really happened that summer. In fact, I'm still trying to forget. I finally walked in the door of my apartment after a long day of work at the office to hear another ringing telephone. I kicked the heels off my sore feet and made it to the phone just in time.

"Sherri, have you talked to your sister," my mom asked. I could hear the frustration in her voice.

"No, I just walked in. What's going on?"

"Nothing, she is just looking for somebody to watch the kids while she's at work. I'm too tired to be running after them tonight."

"I'll watch them mama but I hadn't heard from her yet...Somebody is at the door, I bet it's her."

"Okay sweetheart, call me later"

I almost started to turn off the lights and act like I wasn't home. However, I knew if I didn't agree to watch the kids she would hassle my mom into she finally gave in.

"Hey sis…I love you," she greeted me with a tone indicating she wanted something.

"Yes, I'll watch them."

"That was easy," she stated dropping the honey voice.

Renee promised to be back by eleven and rushed out the door before I could ask if she had fed the kids. My sister has three children and doesn't get help from either of their fathers. Terra, 10, and Michelle, 6, have the same father, but she hasn't said who the father of 2-year-old Derrick is. I'm not sure she actually knows.

I tossed a salad together and ordered a pizza. Derrick waddled into the kitchen with an adorable smile and a rancid odor signaling a diaper change. True to Renee's M.O., there were no Pull-Ups in his diaper bag. I cleaned him up and got a pair of underwear for him to wear long enough to ride to the store. I knew that I wouldn't see the money that I spent but what else could I do. My phone rang at the check-out line and before I even looked at the caller ID I remembered that Tammy was supposed to bring Janise over today. I occasionally watch the kids for her so she can have some alone time. She never asks me but she deserves it.

"You didn't forget I was coming today did you?" Janise gently inquired.

I assured her I didn't and told them to wait for me at the apartment. When I pulled into the parking lot of my apartment complex, Janise was standing out in the breezeway. With her hair blowing in the wind she looked as if she was posing for Teen magazine. Her almond shaped eyes and beautiful skin made her look like a model yet she didn't seem to recognize her own beauty. Tammy and Roderick were sitting on the stairs; Roderick bursting with energy and Tammy looked as if all hers had been drained from her. Once we were spotted, Janise and Rod ran to meet us.

"Hey beautiful and hello handsome," I greeted them.

"Hey Sherri; tell Roderick he is not staying," Janise forcefully pleaded. I promised her a girl's night since she was at a stage seeking solace from sisterhood.

"But Derrick is here!" he shouted.

"I know but he's a baby. You don't want to be stuck with a bunch of girls and a baby, do you?" I asked hoping my reverse psychology would work.

"Come on sweetie we are going to do something just me and you, remember?" his mom chimed in before he could feel unwanted.

"You want to go see the new Disney movie?"

"Yeah," he replied excitedly, my house no longer a temptation. I gave the girls my key so they could open the apartment and I could have a minute to catch up with Tammy.

"I'm so glad Janise had a chance to get up with you. I swear I haven't seen that girl smile in weeks."

"Really? What's been going on?" I asked as I took a seat next to her on the step.

"I don't know. One day we are fine and the next thing I know she is not talking to me. She acts like everybody is against her and she is carrying the whole world on her back. Kids just don't know how good they have it sometimes."

"Is she having a problem at school?" I suggested.

"Well her grades are fine but one of her teachers, Ms. Fuller, is concerned that she is always by herself and is always getting into it with the other kids. She doesn't know why, but like I said Janise doesn't tell me anything. Maybe she will open up to you."

"We'll see… How is everything going with your ex? He isn't still riding past your house is he?"

"No, at least I haven't seen him. I really think he's given up stalking me since he is with his new girl. You know she is supposed to be pregnant."

"You gotta be kidding ! Do the kids know yet?"

"I haven't told them yet. But my thing is, he just does pay child support now, how is he going to take care of three children. Then again it's not because he doesn't have money he just wants me to come crawling back to him."

"Well maybe things will be different now that he is with someone."

"I hope so. What's up with you and Alexis? You went overboard bringing up what happened in college. We all helped her out because she is our friend not so we can throw it at her each time we have a disagreement."

"I know; I've just been on edge lately. I'm going to apologize later."

"And what was she talking about that happened our junior year?" she inquired.

"Who knows," I brushed off the question and stood to go inside.

Tammy

Rod was fast asleep in the back of my Sonata on the way home from the movie theater. Janise had called to say good night and to tell me about the great fun she was having with Sherri. Soon I was pulling into my driveway and Rod was so deep in sleep he didn't budge at my repeated urgings for him to wake. I struggled to carry all fifty pounds of him into the house which felt like dead weight. On my way up the walkway, I noticed the same black jeep parked across the street with the lights out that I had noticed a few nights ago. A dark figure approached as I fumbled to find my keys and I was glad that I finally bought mace for my keychain. Just in time I aimed it at the intruder just as he approached my porch.
"Whoa it's just me" Kenny, my soon to be ex-husband, said identifying himself.
"What are you doing here?" I demanded still gripping my mace.
"I was waiting up to see my little man, but I see he is knocked out. Long night I see."
"Yeah, well like you said he is knocked out so…"
"Yeah, so what are y'all doing out so late." he asked in a joking fashion but I was sill not at ease with the question.
"Look, I'm not going to sit here and get the third degree from you. All this checking up you are doing on me, you need to save for

your new girlfriend. I need to put him to bed; goodnight," I asserted and unlocked the door.

He grabbed my arm to stop me from going in. I was just about to spray but he let me go.

"Wait, don't be like that; I just want to make sure my family is all right; that's all. Besides, I came here to drop off some money. I know I haven't been doing much lately but that is about to change."

"Did you get a promotion or something?" I asked wondering what caused this new change of attitude.

"Nah, my partner needs a little help with his business so I do a couple of odd jobs to earn some extra cash. So, whatever my kids need you just let me know and I got you."

He reached in his pocket and pulled out a roll of money and gave it to me.

"Thanks," I whispered still in shock.

"Tammy, you know I'm a lot different than I used to be,"

"That's good for your new girl," I interrupted him.

"We aren't even together anymore; she was lying about being pregnant just so I could be with her."

"Whatever, I have to go put him to bed; he's getting heavy."

"Why don't you let me take him up for you?" he asked his eyes still holding the sparkle that drew me to him in high school.

"I got it, good night," I said shutting the door before he could protest. I went upstairs and put Rod into the bed and then checked the messages. Stephanie called several times so I decided to call her back.

"What's up; you sounded upset on the message," I asked.

"Bradley and I had an argument. I need to get out for a little while. Is it okay if I stay the night?"

"Of course."

She showed up about ten minutes later. Her eyes were caked with make up in a failed attempt to hide that she had been crying.

"Where's J.B.?" I asked noticing Rods play pal wasn't lagging behind her as usual.

"He's staying the night at my mom's. I was going to go over there myself but I don't want to hear her mouth. She never liked Brad anyway."

"Is everything okay? What happened?"

"It will be, but we both need some time to cool down. I really don't want to talk about it."

"I understand," I told her not wanting to press the matter. "You can sleep in the pull out bed in the den; I'll get you some fresh sheets."

Sherri

My sister didn't pick up the kids until one in the morning. That's why I don't like keeping the kids for Renee because she never picks them up on time. I don't mind watching them while she works but I am not going to baby-sit so she can hang with her friends all the time.

After Tammy came to pick up Janise, I called Tyler to see if we could get together but he didn't answer. I hoped he wasn't upset that I didn't make it to a get together at the new condo last night. He put it together at the last minute and I had already promised Janise she could come over. I tried Kina next to see if she and Alexis went to Tyler's.
"How was the movie?" she asked.
"It was good, I took Janise out to eat afterwards but she seemed a little stressed."
"It's good you are so involved with her; I'm available too if you ever want to put something together."
"Did you make it to Tyler's party last night?" I asked hoping she could give me some insight on his mood.
"Yeah, I met up with Alexis and we rode together."
"She still mad?"

"A little but she promised to drop it. She thinks you blew up because of the whole rent thing. I was correct to assure her that you wouldn't let money get between us, right?" Kina asked.

"Of course, I just let my emotions get the best of me. I'm going to talk to her."

"Good. We missed you last night."

"Me too! Tyler and I hadn't had a chance to talk lately; I'm afraid where things are going with us."

"Why would you say that?" she asked concern seeping through the line.

"Like I said, we haven't been communicating lately. In fact, his last minute invitation was the first time we had spoken in a while. I know we are supposed to slow things down but I feel like he is pulling away. If he wanted to break up I wished he'd say that instead of dragging me along."

"Maybe he's just been busy. Have you tried talking to him about how you are feeling?"

"It's hard to when I can't catch him on the phone. I don't know, maybe I'm overreacting."

"I can't say for sure because you two are in the relationship, I'm just looking in from the outside but I don't think you have anything to worry about."

"What's up with you and Micah?" I asked shifting the focus off of my troubles.

"I hadn't talked to him lately; I'm tired of checking for him. If he wants to be with me he knows my number."

"I feel you. I love Tyler but I refuse to follow behind him while he figures out what he wants to do."

Alexis

I walked into the back door of my new apartment after taking a trip to the grocery store and saw another envelope addressed to me on the floor. I walked past it and the unpacked boxes in the dining room and crossed into the kitchen to sit my bags down. I couldn't believe that Sherri drove all the way here to leave me another note. While I put my groceries away the note haunted my thoughts reminding me of how childish my friend was being. I could understand her being upset but I don't know why she would sweat me like I wasn't going to pay her the money. I started to call her and tell her a thing or two about herself, but I decided to go see her in person. I grabbed up her little note and headed to Greensboro. Adrenaline pumped through my veins as I closed the door to my Taurus and headed up her sidewalk. As I knocked on the apartment door with fists wet from sweat, I started to lose my edge. I waited in anticipation, heart racing, ready for her to open the door. Just when I thought she wasn't coming, the door opened.

"What's up Ale…"

"Here's your money," I said cutting her off. "Now I don't owe you a thing," I said forcefully.

"Okay, I wasn't really worried about it. I know you got caught up with the move. You wanna come in?" she asked.

Her light-hearted manner threw me off but I didn't show it.

"I couldn't tell with you leaving me 'reminder notes' like I wasn't going to pay you," I said walking in the apartment behind her. "Here is your key."

"What are you talking about? I haven't left you any notes," she said as she sat down on the couch, gesturing for me to do the same.

"You are the only person I owe money to. You mean to tell me that you didn't leave me a note with my mail and under my door today?"

"Oh… I found that envelope under the door and placed it with your mail. But, what is this about money?"

"I don't know. I got another one under my door today," I said as I reached in my purse and got the envelope. I read it aloud:

> You are late. Now the price is doubled.
>
> Pay up or expect a little motivation.

"Oh my gosh, Alexis. You better take that to the police."

"I don't know who it could be," I said dumbfounded. "Sherri, I'm sorry I came in here accusing you."

"And I'm sorry for blowing up at you the other night."

I was relieved that she wasn't being petty but then I was afraid of whoever thinks I owe them something and that they know where I live. She assured me that she wasn't taking it personally and I started to feel the connection we had before the rift that came with my move.

"You better go to the police before 'Cousin Vinny' comes looking for you."

I gave an uneasy chuckle. "I guess you're right."

"You want me to come with you?"

"Nah, I have to pick Trina up from the doctor in a minute," I mumbled as I stood to leave. I stared blankly into space for a moment contemplating who could be behind the notes.

"Well, call me and let me know what happens. By the way, how is your mom doing?"

"She's doing a little better. I've been back and forth with her to the doctor and getting medicine. They'll give her a pill to treat one thing and then she'll have to go back and get something else treat the side effects of the first medication. You know how it goes."

The ride from Sherri's apartment was a blur. I couldn't imagine who would come at me like that. I went to the police station to file a report and they said that a detective would contact me to ask some questions. By the time I left I was more than late picking up Trina.

"Everything okay," Trina asked as she plopped in the car.

"Yeah, nothing I can't handle. How's my niece?"

"Good, I'm ready for her to come on out," she answered as my phone rang. I nodded in agreement and then answered the phone.

"Ms. Moretti, this is Detective Andrew Pierce. I got your information and the notes. We dusted it for prints but paper is hard to pick up on. Are you sure you don't owe anyone, or had a fallout with anyone recently?"

"I'm sure. Like I said I don't know who it could be." I fastened my seatbelt and signaled Trina to do the same. Slowly, I exited the parking lot as I listened intently to the detective.

"Well, it's probably just a mix-up."

"A 'mix-up'? Then how did they know where I live? I just moved into my apartment," I argued frustrated at his light-hearted approach to the situation.

"I understand. We will have a car patrol your neighborhood but you should be fine. Be sure to call me if there are any more incidents."

I slammed the phone shut. I couldn't believe his nonchalant attitude. I just hoped that if there was an "incident" that I would be in a position to report it. After everything that happened in college, I vowed not to get caught up in any more drama.

"Are you sure everything is okay," Trina asked noticing my state of frustration and confusion.

"I'm fine, I got a couple of anonymous letters in the mail and I was talking with a detective about it but everything is under control, it's probably just a mix-up," I assured her not wanting to get her involved.

"Oh my god! Were they threatening you," she said and immediately I regretted mentioning it to her.

"Not really… look don't you get all worked up over it; I don't want my niece coming out with eleven fingers and 9 toes," I kidded.

She laughed, "As long as you're good. Let me know if anything else happens."

"I will," I lied. "You come up with any names yet?"

"I was thinking about Alexia Niccole Moretti, like you and your brother."

I dropped Trina off and headed to my mom's house. As I entered the home I was met with the smell of food cooking. I headed in the kitchen to see Lex stirring pots on the stove.

"I'm surprised you can cook," I teased announcing my entrance.

"I do a little something," he said flashing his trademark smile. Like me, he has hazel eyes and smooth caramel skin. "Lexie, I wanna holla at you about something," Lex said motioning for me to follow him outside on the back porch. "Trina said you got some anonymous notes."

"Yeah, but I don't think it's a big deal," I answered surprised that she leaked the message so quickly.

"What did the notes say exactly?"

"The first one said I want my money and the second one said it was doubled and that I was going to get some motivation, whatever that means."

"You still got the notes?" he prodded.

"No. The police kept them."

"You went to the police? I wish you would have talked to me first."

"Well I didn't know what to do. I don't want you getting in to trouble over this thing. Besides they said it's probably just a mix-up; unless you know something about the money or who sent it?"

"You did what you had to; I just don't like anybody messing with my little sister. But if you get anymore let me check it out, a'ight?"

"Okay," I replied.

Mama stepped outside at the tail end of the conversation.

"What's going on?" she asked.

"Nothing much, just catching up," Lex answered her.

"How you doing Mama?" I asked, following her back inside.

"I'm doing. How long are you here for?"

"Well I have to get ready for work; you need anything."

"I need to get some things from the store but it can wait."

"I can get them for you Ma," Lex volunteered.

"Thank you baby, let me make you a list."

"Well, I'm off to work. Love you, Ma," I said reaching down to hug her. She still smelled like Vick's vapor rub and baby powder.

"I love you too," Lex said sarcastically putting me in the choker.

"Yeah, yeah," I said pushing him off. My phone rang as I headed outside. I looked at the caller ID and saw Isaiah's name on the screen.

"You are hard to reach," he spoke lightly as if we were to just pick up where we left off.

"I've been busy. I'm on my way to work now."

"I just wanted to call to see how you were? I haven't talked to you since you moved."

"Yeah, like I said; I have a lot going on right now."

"I understand. Anyway, I have tickets for the Alicia Keys concert; I thought you might want to go."

"I guess I can make time for Alicia."

Initially, I had no intentions of continuing things with Isaiah but I could suffer another evening with him if it meant seeing my girl live.

I walked into Glam and put up my jacket in the storage closet. When I reentered the main part of the store I saw Micah and another female at the clearance rack. I ducked around the corner so I could take a clear picture without being noticed and quickly sent it to Kina.

Chapter 3

Kina

Just as I was starting to push my doubts aside and believe Micah's declaration about the seriousness of our relationship, I get a picture from Alexis with him boo'd up with some chick at Glam. I was already running behind for work, but emotion took over and I punched his number in my cell phone and paced around my living room floor. Each ring boosted my anger and I was ready to go off on him. The voice mail clicked on and his smooth and sultry voice calmly let me know that he was unavailable and assured a return call which irritated me even more.

Unwilling to let it go I tried once more just to get the same message. Frustrated, I grabbed my laptop and headed to work. My explorer sped down Elm Street on the way to the office. I quickly made my way to my desk avoiding eye contact and conversation. Micah's cousin was supposedly taking him to a basketball game at UNCG. But now I know the game was me. The thought regenerated my frustration and I tried his number again. This time I left a message for him to call me as soon as he got the message. Instead of starting on my story, I looked at the girl with him in the photo in my phone. She had a long pony tail, probably a weave, and looked like she was about a size 4 or 6. I wondered if that was why he stood me up. I would rather be her myself. Before I lost myself to tears I left the Journal brushing past anyone searching for answers to my abrupt departure. Alexis called me as I was headed to the car.

"Did he say who she was," she asked.

"I couldn't get him on the phone. Is he still at the store?"

"No, he left before I could confront him."

"I had to leave work it's just getting to be too much. I need to go to the gym to relieve some of my pent up energy and emotions."

"Okay, call me if you need to talk."

I changed clothes at home, no need in using the locker room at the gym if I didn't have to. Sherri called a few times but I ignored it and continued my work out session. After more than an hours worth of exercise I went to the grocery store to pick something up for dinner.

"What's up Kina," I heard someone say as I was selecting a cucumber for my salad.

I turned around to see Tyler in his Wake Forest sweat suit. He looked as if he just woke up.

"Oh, hi Tyler. I see those parties are finally getting to you," I mentioned noticing his bum outfit and muffled hair.

"I wish…I've been up all night studying for my internal medicine exam and my rotation hours are crazy. I'm surprised you don't have plans tonight."

"Yeah, well."

"Everything okay?"

"Other than finding out my boyfriend is cheating on me, everything is good," I confided.

"I hate to hear that. His loss."

"Whatever..." I said not wanting to talk about it anymore. The bruise was still fresh and I was trying to sort my feelings out.

"Seriously, you're a good girl. I don't see why anyone would step out on you."

"Well. I need to get dinner ready, I guess I'll see you around."

"What are you cooking?"

"Spaghetti and salad, nothing special."

"Sounds better than hot pockets," he said as he showed me his dinner.

"I'll save you a plate," I laughed.

Alexis

I was sitting at my desk at WSJ and I received a text message from Kina. I hadn't talked to her since the incident with Micah at Glam and I needed to get up with her. I asked her to come over and she replied that she would. I gathered the articles I was proofreading and got ready to leave.

"You gone for the day," Eugene, sports writer and assistant editor, asked as I was leaving my cubicle.

"Yeah, I was supposed to be off a half hour ago."

"Aww," he replied.

"Don't be so disappointed. I finished preparing the notes you asked for."

"Oh, I'm not worried about work; I wanted to talk to you before you left."

"Really," I said as I paused to hear what he had to say. It was then I noticed his dark brown eyes and I got lost in them for a moment.

"I noticed that you keep to yourself a lot. I never see you at the afternoon luncheons in the break room."

"Well, I just started. Plus, I'm just an intern."

"You'd still be welcome. You know, with anyone else I wouldn't care so much but I was hoping that I could get to know you better."

"Is that so? Well, I'm pretty busy," I said fumbling my keys, "I doubt that I'll have the time."

"How about lunch? You have to take it anyway and it's not intruding into your 'personal time.'"

I sucked my teeth thinking about his offer, "Okay, I could do lunch," I finally replied.

"I'm looking forward to it. How about tomorrow?"

"Sounds good," I said turning to leave. I knew I shouldn't have accepted his offer but it was something about him that I couldn't turn down. I felt a little dishonest since I just went out with Isaiah again but we just aren't hitting it off. He seems like he's trying too hard and I haven't taken any of his calls since the concert. As I headed out the building my phone rang.

"Hey cuz," Missy greeted me.

"What's up?"

"Not much. You think you can watch Miyah and Miguel tonight? I'm going out with K.D."

"Who is K.D.?"

"You remember, dude I was telling you about with the chain."

"Oh 'bling bling'. Girl you ain't gotta play yourself with an ODB looking dude for some bread. I could give you a loan or something." I joked remembering her description of him when we were shopping for baby gifts.

"You got jokes. It's not like that, though. He's good people. And, I said his chain distracted me, not blinded. He's fine girl."

"Whatever, a friend is meeting me at my house but I guess I can watch them. What time?"

"I was hoping I could drop them off in about an hour."

"Okay, I'll see you then."

Hopefully, I haven't set myself up tonight. I've only seen Missy's children in brief increments yet I agreed to watch them. When I pulled into the parking lot of my apartment complex I saw Kina in her car.

"Why didn't you use your key?" I asked as I walked to her. By then she had got out of her car and we both walked upstairs to my apartment.

"I just got here. Besides you gave me a key in case of an emergency."

"Oh, I wouldn't have minded," I assured her as I unlocked the door.

We both put our bags on the table by the door and I hung up my keys.

"How was your day?" Kina asked.

"Interesting," I smiled. She followed me into the kitchen and had a seat at the table.

"Is that so?"

"Yeah, I got to work with Eugene today," I revealed piquing her interest.

I pulled out the ingredients I needed to make tacos and grabbed an apron since I still had on my work clothes.

"And," she eagerly replied.

"He's nice," I stated.

"That's it."

"What do you want me to say? He was nice, I only saw him for a moment."

"Yeah, okay." She got up and fixed herself a glass of lemonade.

"How are you doing? Micah still calling?" I asked.

"He's called a couple of times but I haven't answered."

"Good. I don't think he's right for you. You can do better."

"Yeah, I hope so."

"I know so," I replied as I turned and gave her a smile. She weakly smiled back.

"Have you spoken to Sherri," she asked.

"Yeah, I have been getting these notes about paying back money I owe and I thought it was Sherri tripping about the rent. I rushed over to tell her off just to find out it wasn't her."

"So if it wasn't her who was it?"

"I don't know. The good thing is me and Sherri made up."

"Yeah, but you need to go to the police."

"I have, they are brushing it off as some kind of mistake. But I'm not sure."

"You don't think it has anything to do with what happened in college do you."

"I hope not."

"Maybe it's nothing." She tried to assure me. There was a knock at the door that startled us. Then I remembered Missy was bringing her kids over and went to let her in. She had a dress painted on her with her trademark heels holding a sleeping Miyah.

"Where's Miguel," I asked.

"With his dad for a change. Thank you for watching her."

"No problem. You can lay her on the chair for now," I said gesturing her to the pull-out chair in the living room. I went a got a sheet to cover her with.

"I should be back in a couple hours," she promised.

"Missy this is my girl Kina," I introduced her as she walked out of the kitchen.

"Nice to meet you," Kina greeted her extending her hand.

"You too," she agreed shaking her hand. "Well, I hate to run but I'm late."

I walked Missy to the door then ran into the kitchen to check my sauce.

"Did you see that dress," Kina asked walking back into the kitchen.

"Yeah, no comment." I replied. I dropped the ground meat in the pan. Kina started putting together a salad.

Just as we fixed our plates there was another knock at the door. I opened the door to see Lex and Ka$h.

"What's up Sis?" Lex greeted.

"What's up?" I asked opening the door for him to come in. They came in and remained standing by the doorway.

"I was just leaving the studio and I wanted to swing in and speak. You met my man, Ka$h?"

"Yeah, we've met," I replied giving a forced smile and wave.

"I was on my way home and I wanted to stop by to see if you could take Trina to the store tomorrow while I'm at work so she can pick up some clothes. She is all upset about how much weight she gained and concerned that she won't be able to fit anything once she drops baby girl. I swear one minute that girl is joking around and then the next thing I know she's crying about something."

"I'm sure it's just the hormones from being pregnant. I'll call her tomorrow to see what time she wants to go."

"Cool. I knew I loved you for something," he kidded.

"No problem; I don't mean to rush you, but I have food cooking."

"We can see that," Ka$h replied sarcastically and I remembered my apron now stained with sauce.

"Funny," I replied annoyed. Kina walked into the living room where we were standing.

"It looks good on you," he commented.

"Anyway," Lex loudly interrupted, "we gone head out. I'll see you tomorrow."

"Who is your friend?" Ka$h asked now setting his eyes on Kina.

"This is Kina," I introduced her and she walked closer to where I was standing.

"Hi," was all she offered.

"Well it was nice seeing the both of you," he complimented as Lex ushered him out.

Sherri

It was 7:30 and I was already running late for dinner. I was supposed to be meeting Tyler at his mom's house but my sister hasn't come to get her kids yet. Renee was supposed to pick the kids up after work last night and she never showed up. I have been calling her cell and her house phone and she hasn't returned any of my calls. I took Terra and Michelle to school this morning and dropped Derrick off at the daycare center. The director called me at closing because Renee didn't come pick them up. I couldn't believe she was pulling this again so she could have a free weekend. I got dressed as soon as I got back home hoping she would turn up soon but I'm still waiting. Before I could call Tyler to let him know what was going on, the phone rang.

"Are you on your way? Everyone is asking about you," Tyler asked anxiously.

"No, my sister never came to pick up the kids and I can't reach her."

"Can your mom watch them long enough for you to have dinner?"

"No, she's sick. I could kill Renee; I have really been looking forward to coming because we hadn't seen much of each other lately," I whined.

"Yeah, I know. Whatever, I'll just tell them you couldn't make it, again. I'll call you later."

He didn't waste time hanging up. I couldn't blame him for being upset; I have stood him up a lot recently because of my sister and her kids. I had hoped he would be more understanding, though.

"When is mommy coming? Daddy is supposed to pick us up," Terra asked.

"I don't know sweetheart… Do you want to call your dad and see what time he's coming," I said not saying too much about her mother. I didn't want to bad mouth her to them.

"He wants to talk to you," Terra said handing me the phone so I could talk to her Dad.

"Where is Renee?" he asked, obviously frustrated.

"I hadn't talked to her since she went to work," I said not revealing everything; I didn't want to start any drama between them.

"Oh, I'll be by to get my girls in a few."

Their father, Tommy, lived just outside of Greensboro city limits in High Point which is only about fifteen minutes away so I was hoping that I could make it to the dinner party and take Derrick with me. But, a "few" turned out to be several hours. Tommy finally arrived in a black, 2009 Lincoln MKS. The music was up so loud that the bass rocked the furniture inside my apartment. He hopped out of the car wearing a Sean John jogging suit, a long, gold chain that said "Get Guap," and a gold and diamond grill in his mouth. I wondered how he couldn't afford to help my sister out with the kids.

"Have your sister call me as soon as she gets in."

"Okay," was all I could get out before he hopped in the car with the girls and drove off. Immediately I got a bad feeling about the girls being with him but I dismissed it hoping he wasn't as bad as my sister made him out to be. Since I couldn't make in time to go to the dinner I called Kina over. She stopped by not long after I called.

"Did you work today?" I asked noticing how casually she was dressed. She had on a pair of Levi's and a t-shirt.

"Do I look that rough?" she joked checking out her outfit.

"You know what I mean. How's everything going?"

"Good, I left work a little early and went to the gym. I'm trying to go at least three times a week. I need to do something about this weight I've been gaining.

"You look good," I assured her wondering what mirror she had been looking into. I would change places with her any day. My shape is nice enough for me and Tyler so I haven't been in a rush to shed the extra pounds.

"So what have you been up to?" I asked not feeding her pity.

"Not much. I went to see Alexis yesterday to get out of the house. I was surprised to hear from you tonight; I thought you were having dinner with Tyler and his mom."

"I was supposed to but you see I got stuck with the kids again," I told her motioning towards Derrick's baby bag on my kitchen table. We both made our way to the living room and took a seat next to each other on the sofa.

"What did Tyler say?"

"Not much, he was upset that I couldn't make it. I thought that he would be more understanding."

"Well I can't say that I blame him."

"So, you are taking his side?"

"No. I'm just saying, y'all are always busy and every time he reaches out to you always stand him up."

"You make it sound like I'm flaking on him. I hate that I missed going too, but what was I supposed to do."

"I feel you; I was just saying you have to look at it from both sides."

"I guess…It's just that he's not as affectionate as he used to be and whenever he does ask me out it seems forced, like it's routine…I wonder if it's because I've gained some weight myself," I speculated then tugged at my shirt outlining my frame.

"I highly doubt it, Tyler isn't that petty. I think you should get together and talk. Maybe he feels you're pulling away from him since you are always busy."

"I don't know. Maybe I could go to the gym with you, aren't you allowed to take a guest with you."

"That would be great," she replied enthusiastically but still sounded as if she was feigning interest.

"How's everything going with Micah?"

"Don't even bring his name up," she huffed then rolled her eyes.

"What happened?" I asked grabbing the pillow next to me and rested my arms on it in my lap.

"Alexis saw him in the store with some chick buying some clothes. I confronted him about it but he said it wasn't him even though she sent me the pic."

"I swear men will hold on to a lie until the grave."

"He can keep trying to convince himself but I'm not falling for it."

"Well forget about him; he aint worth it."

"I know right. I met this guy the other day. He gave me his number but I didn't do anything with it. Now that Micah is tripping I might take him up on his offer."

"Offer for what?"

"A date. Chick, what else would I be talking about?"

"I don't know. You been a little wild lately," I joked doing an imitation of a 'round-up' with my hand and riding an imaginary horse.

"You know you need to stop," she said laughing.

"Me, you were the one all up on Pablo at the Mexican restaurant!"

"Carlos," she corrected me. "And I was just playing with him. Anyway, where are the girls?"

"Tommy came and picked them up earlier. Derrick is asleep upstairs."

"You're sister at work or something."

"No, out running the streets as usual. She better not show up with any more babies."

Tammy

It was busy at work today so I called to see if Stephanie wanted to go out for lunch to take a break from all the madness. We both decided to grab a quick bite at the restaurant down the street.

"How is everything; I haven't really seen you since that night at my house," I asked after we were seated and placed our drink orders.

"I'm good. I've been meaning to call you about what went down. The whole argument started because I got a phone call from Jonathan Sr."

"What? I thought you hadn't spoken to him since J.B. was born."

"I haven't, that's why I was shocked to hear from him. Anyway, he said that he was sorry about running out on us and he wants to be in his life. I told him that I had to warm J.B. up to the idea because we've never really talked about his dad before."

"He's never asked?"

"He has but I've always told him that he's just gone. So, now I don't know how he's going to take it."

"You still haven't told him?"

"No, I wanted to talk to Brad about it first and he flipped. He said that he didn't think it was a good idea after all this time. Brad apologized for the whole thing once we sat down and talked about it."

"So y'all are good?"

"Yeah I guess. I mean, we made up but things have been different between us since then. It's like he still doesn't trust me."

The waitress came to take our orders and we sat a moment in silence. Even though there was no communication I could tell being here was like a therapy for her.

"You think y'all are still ready for marriage?" I asked hoping she had given up on the idea. I still thought it was too soon; especially, now with the wild card Jonathan was throwing at her.

"I hope so; I love him. He loves me," she said and her phone rang. She stepped out to take the call so I asked the waitress for a 'to go' box for our food so we wouldn't be late getting back for work.

"That was Brad now," she said as she came back to the table.

"Is everything okay?"

"Yeah. He was just worried because I wasn't at my desk when he called. So what's up with you?"

"Tired; I've been working over time every day this week. Now that Kenny has been helping out more I'll probably cut back."

"That's a shocker."

"I know. I just hope he's not trying to slide his way back in."

"Why not? He might have learned his lesson. I'm sure he loves you and the kids."

"I don't doubt his love but I just can't take that chance. I admit it's hard, though, with him stepping up lately. He is reminding me of the boy I met in high school."

"I knew you weren't as tough as you pretend to be. Girl, everybody has a weak spot and I think Kenny is yours."

"Yeah he's nice to reminisce about but I outgrew Kenny a long time ago," I pointed out.

We chatted for a little while before we had to go back.

Talking about Kenny at lunch had me distracted and I hardly got any work done that afternoon. I was too busy thinking about how I got wrapped around Kenny's finger like the red on a candy cane. Kenny was the star quarterback at Dudley High School. He was brown skinned and he kept his head clean cut with waves in his hair. Not the wet kind but the waves guys get when they use blue Bergamot hair grease, brush 500 times before they go to bed, and sleep in a Doo Rag. Just like too many young girls, I worried too much about what I didn't have and compared my self to the other girls and became insecure with myself.

"I never seen you around here before; are you new here?" Kenny asked me one day at lunch.

When I realized he was talking to me it was like a vacuum sucked all the oxygen from my area and left me speechless.

"I said are you new here?" he repeated.

"No, I've been here since freshman year," I replied barely above a whisper.

"I'm Kenny."

"I know… My name is Tamika but everybody calls me Tammy."

"Okay, Tammy. You got a date for the spring dance?"

"Not yet," I answered as my heart beat sped up in excitement.

"Now you do," he answered as he got up to leave the table. "Talk to you later, Tammy."

I ended up getting pregnant that year and we were an instant family. He got a job once I had the baby and we got married after graduation and moved into our own apartment. I thought that we were set but reality soon slapped me in my face and brought me back to the real world. Kind of like Stephanie did when she walked into my office interrupting my flashback.

"Hey girl you okay," she asked closing the door behind her.

"Yeah I'm good. Just thinking about some things," I said as I shuffled some papers around on my desk.

"What are you doing tonight?"

"I don't know. Brad is going out with his boys tonight. You want to take the kids to the skating rink."

"That sounds good. I know Janise will be glad to get out of the house," I said as I got up from my desk. I needed to take a bathroom break.

"Cool, I'll meet you at your house after work," she said as she headed out. Even though I was only going to be gone a minute I decided to lock up my office.

"Excuse me Ms. James." I turned around to see a young man who looked like he just graduated from high school. I was about to ask him what he was doing here but I noticed his badge that told me he was one of the 'tech' guys.

"Yes," I said shutting the door behind me.

"I have a work order for a computer upgrade."

"Oh, well go on in. I'm headed out now. I don't remember putting in an order."

"I know but the company is upgrading everyone who doesn't have the latest programming."

"No problem." I paused for a minute to make sure I didn't leave anything of value in my office. "How old are you, if you don't mind me asking?"

"I don't; I get that a lot. I'm 25," he said as he switched his clipboard to his other hand, flexing his biceps.

"Well, I'll let you get your work done."

"I'm Kevin, by the way."

"Good to know," I said walking away.

"Ms. James…"

"Please, call me Tammy. I'm not that much older than you."

"I'm sorry Tammy, it's just common courtesy. I didn't take you for more than 22."

"You're sweet," I said getting ready to leave.

"Tammy," he called again before I could leave.

"Yes Kevin," I said trying not to sound annoyed.

"I need to get in, you locked the door."

"I'm sorry," I said blushing in embarrassment.

Alexis

It was awkward at work today; occasional smiles to Eugene yet trying to stay focused on work hoping no one notices. That is exactly why I don't like to get involved with the people I work with. It never fails to become a soap opera scene instead of a professional environment. By the time lunch came around I was starving. I went to the bathroom to check my hair and make-up. My limbs tingled in excitement and I don't know why I was acting like a school girl getting ready for a date; it was obvious that I couldn't pursue anything with Eugene. I did one final look over and stepped back outside.

"There you are; you ready to go," Eugene asked as I rounded the corner.

"Yeah, let me grab my coat. I'll meet you outside"

I went to get my coat and purse and passed Kina along the way.

"Are you going out for lunch too," she asked one eyebrow raised and smile painted on her face.

"Yep," I replied quickly.

"You behave yourself," she joked.

Eugene was standing by his new model Lexus and I decided to ride with him.

"I know this little diner that's close by. The southern food is the best I've tasted."

"Sounds good to me," I answered.

We arrived at the diner in less than five minutes and were seated just as fast. It was a quaint, cozy restaurant. Eugene and I were seated at a booth and I sat across from him. Looking at him from across the table I noticed that he had dimples. I brushed the image out of my head remembering that nothing could jump off between us because of the work situation.

"I'm surprised I never ran across this place," I said breaking the silence.

"After today, I'm sure you will be a regular too. So tell me, have you always lived in Winston?"

"No. My mom and I moved nearby when I was younger. I have been staying in Greensboro with my friend but I wanted to be closer to my mom since she's been having health problems."

"I'm sorry to hear that. Is she doing okay?"

"She's fine now. I just wanted to be able to help her out when she needs it."

"I like that. A lot of people just put their parents in nursing homes and retirement communities. That says a lot about you."

"Like what?" I asked holding back a grin.

"That you are compassionate, brought up the right way, you care about family."

Flattered with the compliment I shifted in the seat.

"Okay, enough about me; what about you? Do you have any family nearby?"

"My family is not too far, they stay in Greensboro. I moved here once I started at Winston-Salem State."

"Get out of here; I'm graduating from WSSU this year!"

"Wow. I was a senior your freshman year. I remember seeing Kina a couple times though."

"Kina is my girl. I've been friends with her and Sherri since college. They were sophomores when I started."

I paused taking in the moment of our unlikely connection. We talked about almost everything. We seem so different with little in common but there was still something about him that made me want to know more The calm and the intense chemistry building with each second that passed started to get to me and I decided to break the silence. "Why did you choose to work at the Journal?"

"I wanted to be a sports writer and they were looking for one when I graduated. So, here I am."

"Just like that, huh. You didn't go through an internship?"

"I interned at High Point Enterprise but they weren't trying to hire another sports columnist so I applied at other papers. I'm glad I took this job though, I like my column plus I got to meet you."

"True, I would hate to rob you of that privilege," I replied jokingly.

"Well, I hate to say it, but it's about time to head back."

"I guess it is; the time just flew by."

"So, when can we do this again?" he asked looking right through me.

"I don't know Eugene, I don't really like work relationships."

"Who said anything about a relationship? I enjoy spending time with you and I was hoping we could get together again."

"I must admit, I like talking to you too."

"So let's not put a label on it. We can just see where our conversations take us."

Kina

I logged off my computer at work and grabbed my gym bag off the floor of my cubicle. I was in a rush since I was late meeting Sherri at the gym. Still I went over to find Alexis to see if she had left yet. "Hey girl," I said catching her attention. She was intently focused on whatever she was typing.

"What's up," she responded.

"I'm on my way to meet Sherri at the gym. We are supposed to get together at her house afterward, you coming?"

"What time?"

"Around 8:30."

"I'll be there."

"Good, I want to hear all about your lunch date."

"There's not much to tell."

"It was that bad?" I asked.

"Nothing like that, it was fine. But we're just friends."

"If you say so, I'll see you at Sherri's."

I waited for Sherri outside the gym for fifteen minutes before I headed in the locker room. I changed my clothes and brought my cell with me in case she called. I made my way to the tread mills but they were all taken, I was about to get on a bike instead.

"You can use this one, I'm getting off," said a tall, light skinned gentleman.

"Thanks," I replied.

"My name is Kyle, I don't think I've seen you in here before, I would have remembered."

"Kina," I said, extending my hand. He shook it firmly but not too hard. "Thanks again." Another guy was headed to the tread mill so I hurriedly got on and started it up. Kyle was still standing at my side staring at me.

"Is something wrong," I asked.

"No, I was getting up the nerve to ask you out. I know a great place around the corner, maybe we can go for dinner after your workout."

"That would defeat the purpose of working out wouldn't it," I replied. "Besides, I'm meeting some friends tonight."

"Hopefully I'll see you here again; maybe we could work out together."

"Maybe," I responded, and my phone rung. Kyle waved as he left so that I could take the call. I paused the machine.

"Hey girl, I'm outside," Sherri stated. I met her and signed her in as a guest. By the time I got back to the machine someone had taken it.

"You want to do the elliptical," I asked.

"Sure," Sherri responded.

"I didn't think you were coming," I said, as we mounted the machines.

"I'm sorry. I had to stay late with a client...I really need to come more often," Sherri said between heavy breaths.

"I don't know if I can do this," Sherri whined after about fifteen minutes on the elliptical.

"We can do the bike if you want," I suggested.

"Girl yeah, I need to work up to this. Who is that guy that keeps staring at us?"

"Where?" I asked looking around for Kyle.

"Over at the weights," she pointed.

"Oh, I don't know," I answered, a little disappointed. It wasn't Kyle but I saw him in the same area talking to another female.

We worked out for another 30 minutes and showered before going over to Sherri's place. Tammy and Alexis were sitting on her stairs waiting for us.

"I thought you said 8:30," Alexis commented as we made our way up the stairs.

"I said around 8:30, it's still in the vicinity. How long have y'all been waiting?" Sherri asked.

"Not too long," Tammy answered.

"Long enough," Alexis replied jokingly.

"At least we came bearing gifts," Sherri responded holding out the pizza boxes.

"Doesn't that defeat the purpose of the work out," Alexis commented.

"Not really, I ate a light lunch and I got veggie pizza for myself," she defended herself.

"I bought a salad," I added not mentioning that I urged her to stay away from fast foods. I sat the food down on the counter and took my turn washing my hands.

"You have anything to drink?" Tammy asked.

"Yeah, it's some diet sodas and juice in the fridge," Sherri answered.

"You mean to mix with the drinks," Tammy laughed, "It's been a rough week."

"What's going on," I asked.

"Nothing specific. Between Stephanie coming to me with her drama and going up to Janise's school, it's been a long week."

"I have some red wine."

"That'll work."

"Are you and Eugene going out again," I asked Alexis anxious to get the scoop on today's lunch date.

"Maybe," she said shooting me daggers with her eyes.

"What happened to Isaiah?!" Sherri inquired.

"Nothing, I haven't talked to him since the concert."

"You've been hanging around Kina too long," Sherri kidded. "She teaching you how to be a player?"

"No, I'm teaching her. Besides, Eugene and I are just friends."

"For now," I added.

We headed into the living room with our plates and glasses. I was glad to have the gang together again. It brought back memories of the late nights we spent in college.

"How is Tyler," Tammy asked after we finished eating.

"Okay, I guess. I hardly get to see him, and with everything with my sister I see him even less."

"She still hasn't shown up," I asked.

"No, they're with my mom now. She's really starting to tick me off."

"I'm sure she'll turn up soon," Tammy assured.

"I hope so. Anyway, Alexis, you haven't gotten anymore notes have you?"

"Thankfully, no."

"Good, hopefully that will blow over too," Tammy again offered a positive outlook.

"Lord knows I'm not trying to go down that road again," Sherri stated.

"Because, of course we wouldn't want to you to be bothered," Alexis commented while rolling her eyes.

"I'm just saying I don't need any more drama in my life right now," she explained.

"It's not about you right now," Alexis countered.

"How can you say that?" Sherri asked.

"Guys let's just drop it," I jumped in.

"Yes," Tammy agreed. "How many guests can you have at this gym, I need some stress release too."

"I don't know; I'll check."

"Are we still going to play Spades?" Tammy asked.

"Yeah, I hope you and Sherri have been practicing," I teased.

"Well let's finish eating so we can get started," Sherri directed as she got up to take her plate in the sink.

"I'm finished," I stated and got up to follow Sherri in the kitchen.

"You didn't even finish your salad?" Sherri pointed out.

"I'm not that hungry," I replied wondering why she was focused on my diet instead of hers.

"Everything okay," Tammy inquired.

"I'm fine; y'all just hurry up so we can play."

Chapter 4

Sherri

Renee still has not contacted us. Tommy took the girls to school this morning and Mama picked them all up from Child's Haven before the director got suspicious and called family services.

"Your sister is starting to worry me," Mama told me when I went to check on her and the kids. She was in the kitchen preparing dinner and the kids were upstairs.

"I wouldn't stress too much over it Ma," I said as I grabbed a piece of celery off the counter. "She's probably partying with her friends again."

"Yeah, I hope that's all it is." She said as she continued stirring the pots. "You know her manager called me because she didn't show up for work," she said her forehead wrinkling.

"Sometimes she doesn't think before she does things; she can't lose this job and she has three mouths to feed. She'll probably show up with a thousand excuses like she did last time when she ended up pregnant with Derrick," I said not sure if I was trying to convince Mama or myself. I reached to take the lid off one of the pots and she smacked it away.

"Well, I'm not going to work my blood pressure up over it. The kids will be fine over here tonight, but you can pick them up from the daycare tomorrow if Renee hasn't gotten them yet."

"Okay. I'm going to call her friend, Helen, from work to see if she's heard from her," I said as I grabbed a chicken leg before she could stop me. I leaned over to peck her on the cheek, "I'll call you later."

"All right sweetie," she said handing me a napkin.

On my way home I received a call from Tommy. He wanted to know if Renee came and got the kids yet. I avoided answering the question directly because I didn't want to start any custody drama. I decided to drive by Renee's apartment to see if she had been there. Her car was in the parking lot so I pulled in and went to her apartment. I banged on the door but she didn't answer. I used my key to get in calling her name as I entered. The house was silent and I looked around to see if I could find her. The house was tidy and nothing seemed out of place. After my search came up empty, I locked up and headed back to my car. I was still hoping that she was out with some guy but after leaving her apartment I wasn't so sure. Mom called to ask me what I found out from Helen and she insisted that we go ahead and file a missing person's report. I agreed and went ahead to the police station.

The station was relatively empty when I arrived so I hoped that it wouldn't take too long. I entered the building and went to the reception area.

"How can I help you," the receptionist greeted me as I approached the window.

"I want to file a missing person's report."

"Have a seat and an officer will be with you shortly."

I walked over to the seating area and sat down on one of the hard seats. After a few moments of waiting and shifting uncomfortably in my seat I figured that it probably would have been better if I called it in and had an officer come out to my apartment. It wasn't too much longer before a middle-aged police officer came out to take my report. His uniform was neatly pressed but his hair was a little tousled. He took me to an area that afforded a little more privacy but not too much.

"I'm Officer Jenkins. How may I help you today?" he asked as he took a seat behind his desk and picked up a clipboard.

"I'd like to file a missing person's report.

"What is the name of the person that you would like to file a report on?" he asked never looking up from his paperwork.

"Renee Robinson," I answered as I looked to make sure he was writing down the information I was giving him and not working on some other assignment.

"Why do you think that she is missing?" he asked finally looking at me.

"Well, I was watching her children, my nieces and nephew, and she never came to pick them up and she hasn't shown up to work."

"How long has it been since you last had contact with her?" he questioned as if this was a normal routine.

"It was last Thursday; March second I think. Anyway she dropped off the kids that night and I hadn't heard from her since."

"Is it possible that she is just taking a break from the children or work?"

"I doubt it," I answered, ironically irritated that he made my same assumption. "She has never been gone this long."

"What was she wearing when you last saw her?"

"Her uniform, she works at Subway on Summit Avenue."

"Do you know if she made it to work that night?"

"Yes. Her coworker, Helen, said she left with someone in a late model Cadillac."

"Do you know who that could be?"

"No."

"I need a description of your sister, as specific as possible."

"She is a darker complexion than I am but not much, dark brown eyes. She has dark brown hair with blond highlights; her hair comes down to her shoulder. She is roughly 130 pounds, 5'7. I can't really think of anything else."

"That's great. Does she have any scars, tattoos, or any other marks?

"She has a scar on her leg and a tattoo."

"Where are the scar and the tattoo specifically?"

"The scar is on the back of her left leg and she has a tattoo of a butterfly on the back of her right shoulder."

"Do you have a recent photo of her?"

"Yes," I said reaching into my purse.

"You mentioned she has children, what's the relationship like between her and the father."

"Well she's not with the father of her two oldest daughters; I'm not sure who the father of her youngest son is," I answered somewhat embarrassed by the fact that my sister is unmarried with two baby daddies.

"Have there ever been any problems between them?"

"They argue from time to time but nothing serious."

"Is she seeing anyone now?"

"I don't know."

"Were you having problems with her?"

"What is that supposed to mean?" I asked slightly irritated.

""Did you guys have an argument about anything or was she upset with you when she left?"

"No, she was fine."

"Do you know anyone that would want to hurt her?"

"No. I mean she's a people person, she never really got into it with anyone."

"Well, I will file this report and we will contact you if we find out anything. Here is my card; if you think of anything else, give me a call."

Tammy

Kenny asked if he could take the kids this weekend. I hesitated at first but deep down I knew that Kenny would take good care of his kids. Besides he's supposed to be taking them shopping for school clothes. With the kids gone for the weekend I called to see if I could get together with my girls. Sherri wasn't in her office but I got Stephanie on the phone.

"I don't know if I can make it. Brad and I are trying to work things out."

"I thought y'all made up."

"I did too but he is still insisting that I keep J.B. away from his father and Jonathan is pushing even more to see him. He even threatened to take me to court about it. Girl I don't know what to do."

"Well it is his son; he has rights. In the end you have to do what's best for J.B."

"That's what I want but I don't want to mess things up with Brad and I don't know if Jonathan is sincere or not."

"Have you thought about introducing him to J.B. but not telling him it's his father until you know whether he will stick around?"

"I mentioned it but it's hard for me to convince Brad that just because he's back in J.B.'s life that doesn't mean that I want him back."

"I understand that but you can't cheat J.B. out of getting to know his father."

"I know… that's why I want to spend some time together this weekend to talk about it while J.B. is gone."

"Okay girl; I'll talk to you later."

I hung up the receiver and logged on to my laptop. I had a meeting later in the afternoon and I needed to get my portfolio together. For some reason I was having trouble logging in to the network since they upgraded the software. After several failed attempts, I called the extension to technical support. I decided to do some long overdue filing while I waited on someone to come help me. While I was filing my cell phone rang.

"Hey girl," Kina said.

"Hey, what's up?" I answered as I took a seat at my desk.

"Not much; I needed to ask you something. I'm not prying or anything, but did you get back with Kenny after he cheated?"

"Yeah, my mistake," I replied wondering why she wanted to know.

"Did he ever cheat again?"

"Probably; where is all this coming from?"

"Well Micah left me a message earlier. He says that he wasn't serious about the girl he was caught with. He admits he messed up but he wasn't sure how serious we were going to be. He sounds sincere but I'd hate to get burned."

"I don't know what to tell you; all men are different. What did Sherri say about it? She knows him better than I do."

"I hadn't said too much about it to her. You know how she is, once a dog always a dog attitude, still looking for a fairy tale mate."

"True. Well I'm no expert either. You see where my choice in men left me."

"But I take that as a lesson learned. Besides you still got time to make the right choice. You're not old yet."

"Yeah and I'm not looking either. Who wants to jump into family life unless they got one of their own?"

"You never know. Besides you just said all men are different."

"We'll see. Anyway, I said I'm not looking I didn't say I was turning down offers," I joked.

"I know that's right."

"Girl, I'll get back up with you later. The tech guy is here to fix my computer," I said waving the young technician inside my office.

"Hello again. You didn't break your laptop just so you could see me again," he kidded.

"Uh … no. I'm having trouble logging into the network."

"Let me take a look at it," he said looking over my shoulder and I got a whiff of his cologne.

"Here you go," I said pushing the laptop over to the side so he could get a better look without him having to be in my bubble. He tried the same things I did without any luck.

"It may be a problem with the connection in here," he said checking the terminals in my office.

I caught myself looking at how his muscles bulged a little as he traced the wires around the room. I turned to my computer before he caught me staring at him and got the wrong idea. Unable to concentrate I decided to call Sherri again.

"I'm going to step out and make a phone call," I explained as I left my office. I noticed heads turning as I stepped out so I headed to the break room for a little privacy.

"Hey girl; I meant to call you back," Sherri answered the phone.

"What are you doing this weekend?" I asked her.

"I don't have any plans. What did you have in mind?"

"Nothing specific, the kids will be at Kenny's for the weekend so I wanted to take advantage of my free time."

"Cool, let's get together. You must be having a slow day today; you are usually too busy to talk to me at work."

"I know. My laptop is acting up and I had one of the tech guys to come look at it. I needed to take a break because I'm sitting in there thinking of asking him to give me a personal upgrade," I joked around.

"You ought to be ashamed of yourself."

"Why? Because I'm moving on?"

"No because you're married."

"Separated, and soon to be divorced. Would you rather I sniff around Kenny's doorstep."

"No, I just think you should take things one step at a time. Let the papers dry first," she laughed.

"That's easy for you to say. Have you heard from your sister yet?"

"Not yet. I filed a missing person's report a couple days ago."

"I'm sorry to hear that. Hopefully everything is fine… I need to get ready for this meeting. Give me a call after work."

By the time I got back to my office the young technician had left already. He left a note saying what the problem was and he left his a number for me to call if I had any more problems.

Alexis

It was buzzing at the store today. From the moment I walked in I could sense the nerves and excitement from everyone. The owner, Bridgette, was scheduled to come in and evaluate our performance. Even though I've never met her I recognized her as soon as she walked in. She wore designer clothes and a regal presence. She didn't say much while she was there but kept notes in the clip board she carried around. After she walked off I looked around for Missy. I found her outside taking a smoke break.

"I was wondering where you took off to," I said as I met her by the back door.

"Oh, I thought I told you I was heading out," she said in a low tone.

"Are you all right?" I asked.

"Yeah, it's been a long day. You want to go grab something to eat across the street?"

"Sure, let me get my jacket and let them know we're taking lunch." Jerry was still talking with Bridgette so I let one of our co-workers know we were gone.

When I got back outside Missy was by the curb waiting, her head hung low, and I couldn't help but notice something was bothering her.

"You sure everything is all right?" I asked walking up beside her.

"I'm fine. It's just one of those days."

"You think you can finish your shift?"

"Yeah, I'll be fine. Besides we get off in a couple hours and I have tomorrow off."

I let it go and we headed inside the restaurant and ordered two subs and an order of fries.

"You know you were right about Jerry," I said as we sat down with our food hoping to awaken her from her funk.

"What do you mean?"

"He asked me out to dinner last week."

"Why am I not surprised? Have you been by to see the baby yet?" she asked switching the subject; I was surprised she didn't rub it in more.

"Yeah," I replied, "I went to see them at the hospital Saturday. I need to go by the house and see her again."

"Me too, I haven't seen her yet. Do you know how much she weighed?"

"Six pounds nine ounces; I figured she was going to be a small little thing."

"I know. I hate your Pops couldn't see her. It must be killing Lex."

"Yeah it is."

"I can't believe them niggas had the guts to come after Pops. They took care of them though."

"So they did know who shot him?" I said surprised by the information.

"Yeah it was them young Relics hoping to make a come up. Everybody thought Lex was gone take the throne but he passed the torch Big Al's brother and sold the store and came here to be with you. Anyway, are you going over to see Alexia tonight?"

"Yeah… I mean for a little while," I said hoping that she would continue, but I didn't push it. "I can't stay long; I'm going out to dinner with someone."

"Excuse me," she said nearly choking on her food.

"Come on dish it. Who is it? What does he look like? What kind of whip he pushing?" she asked playfully.

"It's not that serious. I'm going out to eat with this guy from the Journal."

"Really?"

"Yeah. Why do you sound so surprised?"

"I'm not. I thought you didn't do work relationships."

"I don't," I replied a little too defensively. "We're just hanging out. Well, we better get back to work," I said getting up to throw away the trash. As if on cue, Eugene called me.

"I gotta take this."

"Okay, I'll meet you inside," she muttered as she departed. I answered once Missy was out of earshot.

"I was thinking," Eugene spoke over the phone, "Instead of going out, why don't you meet me at my place and I can whip us up something?"

"I don't know. One date and you already trying to get me to your place."

"It's not like that. I'm a gentleman."

"Okay. I have to make a stop after work; I can be there around 7:30."

He gave me his address and directions to his place.

Missy and I passed time at the store with conversation but I couldn't get her to divulge anything else about my dad or Lex without sounding too eager. Missy rode with me to go see Alexia and I picked Kina up from the Journal on the way.

Trina answered the door with Alexia in her arms.

"Don't take this the wrong way, but you look a mess," Missy said as we came in.

"I know. I'm so tired. She has been up all night and every time I fall asleep she wakes up."

"She is too cute," Kina complimented.

"Where's Lex," I asked as I took the baby from her.

"Do you even have to ask?"

"What time does he get off?" I asked.

"I'm not sure."

"You want me to stay and watch the baby for a while so you can get some rest," I offered

"That would be great. You sure you don't mind?"

"Of course not" I replied bringing the baby closer to my face relishing in the new baby scent.

"Thanks so much. Her diapers and things are here," she said pointing to the bassinet. "She has a bottle in the fridge and the formula is on the table."

"Just get some rest, we got this," I insisted.

"All right. Thanks y'all," she said as she disappeared into the bedroom. We all took turns holding the baby and changing her. I fixed her a bottle and as soon as she fell asleep my phone rang. The music blared from my purse and I scrambled to turn it off. I looked the caller ID and saw it was Isaiah calling.

"I do not have time for you," I mumbled under my breath.

"Who are you being so rude to," Kina asked.

"Just Isaiah."

"Who is Isaiah," Missy asked raising her eyebrow.

"Nobody really. We were talking before I moved but I'm not interested in him like that."

"I guess not since you already have a dinner date," Missy offered.

"You and Eugene are getting along well," Kina inquired.

"You could say that… We're becoming good friends."

"If you say so, player," Missy joked.

"Whatever," I laughed.

"What's so funny?" Lex asked as he came in the door.

"Nothing, we were just joking around," Missy answered.

"How is my baby girl," he asked as he came in and rubbed Alexia's back as she lay in the bassinet.

"Adorable, she has been asleep the whole time we've been here," Missy answered.

"Where's Trina?" he inquired.

"We made her get some rest to since we are here," I answered.

"Well, I better get a move on. I don't want to stay out too late tonight; I have to work tomorrow."

"Please, you are trying not to be late for your date," Missy said in a mocking tone.

"A date?" Lex said gasping sarcastically.

"Dinner," I replied. "And the sooner I get started the sooner I can get home. Like I said I have work tomorrow."

"Yeah right, you got Jerry wrapped around your finger. You could come in three hours late and he wouldn't say anything except maybe to ask you out again," Missy joked making me regret even telling her.

"That's who you are going out with," Lex asked suspiciously.

"No, I'm going with someone else."

"So, who is Jerry?" Lex asked protectively.

"A manager at Glam; but trust me I'm not interested."

"Well, he sure is interested in you," Missy added teasingly.

"Oh yeah, he giving you a hard time," Lex probed.

"No, Missy is exaggerating," I said reassuringly.

"Missy you keep an eye on my baby-sister," he joked as we said our goodbyes and headed for the door. Wasting no time, I dropped Missy off at Glam so Kina and I could talk. Just as I started to drive Kina to her car, I got a call from Eugene.

"Please forgive me," he said after I picked up.

"Okay... for what?"

"I forgot my frat brother was coming over. I didn't realize it until he showed up at my doorstep."

"That's okay, we can reschedule."

"Thank you for understanding; he came all the way from Virginia. It totally slipped my mind. You had a brother blinded."

"Is that right? Well you have fun and I'll talk to you later."

"Guess I'm not going to dinner after all," I mentioned to Kina who was looking aimlessly out the window.

"Join the group."

"Maybe it's a good thing; we need to hang out more. It may be just what you need to get your mind off Micah."

"Who says I'm thinking about him?"

"You don't have to say it. You've been in a slump since I sent you the picture."

"It's not so much Micah, but men in general. Every guy I've ever been with has cheated on me and I figured it was because no one wanted to be a chubby chaser. But even now that I lost weight…"
I pulled in next to her car and turned off the engine. "Hey, don't start blaming yourself. You are beautiful and he knew what he was getting into when he started dating you. You weren't big when he asked you out and you aren't big now. I won't let you bash yourself because he's an idiot."
"You wouldn't understand. You've never had a problem with your weight or with men."
"Please, I've had my problems too. We all have, it's not us, its men."
"I guess you're right," she replied as if she didn't believe it.
"I know I am," I replied as I took hold of her hand. She gave me a smile but I knew my friend too well. I could tell that something was eating her and for a moment she looked as if she was going to say more.
"I'm tired tonight. I'll call you tomorrow," she said as she exited my car.
Not long after I pulled into my parking lot Missy called. I wondered what she wanted so soon.
"Hey," I answered.
"I hope I'm not interrupting anything."
"No we had to reschedule."

"Oh. Can you talk then?"

"Sure. What's up?"

"You remember K.D. right?"

"Yeah, your sugar daddy."

"Not anymore. We broke up today. I figured it was coming; that's why I was stressed today but I just got off the phone with him and its official."

 "Why? What happened?"

"Well he is seeing some other chick."

"I'm sorry to hear that," I responded wondering how I became the date doctor.

"I mean he's not even answering his phone; I can't believe he gone play me like that," she said stifling tears.

I didn't realize she cared so much; it was probably the money more so than him.

"I wouldn't even sweat it; like you said he's seeing somebody else. It's good you found out early," I comforted her as I hopped out the car and headed to my apartment.

"I guess you are right. I should have seen it coming though. I can't believe I fell for him so fast."

"You said it yourself, you were blinded by the bling," I joked to cheer her up.

I got out my keys to unlock the door and I realized it was already cracked.

"Missy I'm going to call you back; I think someone broke into my house," I said and hung up the phone.

I slowly opened the door to see if anyone was still there. My lamp was knocked down and papers were scattered all over the living room floor. The T.V. was still on the stand and I didn't see anyone, so I walked around to see if anything was missing. I headed towards my bedroom and I noticed that the kitchen drawers were all turned out and the contents were all over the floor. I grabbed my phone and kept going towards my room. I started calling the police but before I could finish dialing someone grabbed me from behind and covered my mouth to keep me from screaming. Immediately I thought about the notes.

Chapter 5

Sherri

This week has been stressful; we haven't heard anything from my sister or the police. My mom is barely holding it together and I'm worried about her heart murmur. With all this excitement and anxiety the doctors put her back on her medicine. Dad is being strong for all of us but I can tell it is getting to him too. I brought the kids home with me to give her a break for the weekend. I called Alexis earlier to see how she has been doing and to get my mind off it but her phone went straight to voicemail. Not long after I hung up Tyler finally called me.

"We need to talk, can you meet me?" he asked.

"I don't know. I just got the kids from mom. You can come over here," I suggested.

"Nah, we can just talk later."

"Well let me see if Tammy is still willing to watch them. I'll call you right back."

Thankfully Tammy agreed because I didn't want to stand him up again. I met Tyler at a Japanese restaurant. When I arrived he was waiting for me by the door.

"Well, hello stranger," he said greeting me with a smile and a hug.
"I already have a table."
"So, how have you been," I asked once we sat down.
"Good. I have been really busy lately at the hospital. I have a new roommate, Jaleel. He's Mr. Hendricks' nephew; he just moved here from South Carolina."
"Oh, so you like the new living arrangements?"
"Yeah he's actually pretty cool. So, what's new with you? You sounded a little upset on the phone."
"Well, I still haven't heard from my sister. I filed a missing persons' report Monday but we haven't heard anything from them yet."
"How have you been holding up?"
"Okay, I guess. I just thought she was off with her friends again; but now..." I paused, unable to complete my sentence.
"I'm sorry to hear that," he replied. He reached across the table and took hold of my hand. It felt nice to be with him for a change.
"What happens if your sister doesn't show up, are the kids going to stay with you or your mom?"
"I don't know. They have been back and forth between us. My mom couldn't take raising them, though, so they would probably be with me."
"Somehow, I'm not surprised," he retorted rekindling the tension that has been building between us.

"What's that supposed to mean."

"Nothing."

"No, say what's on your mind." I said a little agitated by his comment.

"Really, I didn't mean anything by it. Its just that you always have them with you now; I can only imagine how hard it will be for us to get together if you have them full time."

"Well, they're my family; I can't just throw them on my mama or the system."

"I know; I wouldn't expect for you to. Let's hope that it doesn't come down to that."

"Can we just talk about something else? I was looking forward to dinner with you so I could take my mind off all of it. Besides you had something you want talk about."

"Yeah, but in the light of everything it all seems so trivial now."

Tammy

As I was contemplating plans for another child free weekend, Sherri called to see if I could watch the kids. Although reluctant, I agreed because I knew she needed a break. She dropped them off almost immediately, and when I found out it was so she could see Tyler I forgave her. Since I was tied to the house, I decided to call Kina to see if she wanted to come over.

"Hey girl, long time no see," she answered.

"I know right. You want to come over and chill for a little?"

"Yeah sure. My plans got canceled for tonight."

"Mine too," I added.

"Oh, so I was just a second draft pick?"

"Don't sound so offended; I was going to invite you too, maybe."

"Whatever, I'll be there in a few."

I put the girls in Janise's room to watch the television for a while and put Derrick to bed in Rod's room. It wasn't long before Kina was at my door.

"So where's Janise and Rod?" Kina asked as she came in and took a seat.

"With Kenny."

"Uh oh, you think you're grown now."

"Not really. I'm watching the kids for Sherri; she needed a break," I replied and sat next to her on the sofa.

"I know. I talked to her earlier, she sounded worn down. So the kids are with Kenny, does that mean he has finally stopped fighting the divorce?" she asked making herself more comfortable in the chair.

"Surprisingly, yes. He is trying to be in the kids' lives more and I think he's really trying to get his life together."

"Do you think that you could get back with him?"

"I don't think so. Too much has happened between us. Besides I don't know what is going on with him and his new baby's mama."

"I didn't know he had another baby! Do you know her?"

"No. He's not sure if she's really pregnant. He said that they broke up so I don't know what the deal is between them. I didn't ask anything else about it because it's not my business."

"Well if she does have his baby, are you going to let your kids get to know him or her?"

"I don't know. I would like to since they are blood, but I don't know what their relationship is like. I don't want my kids caught up in any drama either. I haven't even told them yet. I want to wait and see how everything goes first."

"I feel you. That's gotta be tough. How do you feel about it? I know that he's done some messed up stuff, but did it hurt that he has another child so soon."

"Well, I still have love for him, but I fell out of love with him a long time ago. Anyway, what were your plans for tonight? Hot date?"

"Something like that, what about you?"

"Well, Sherri and I were going to get up but I told her I would watch Renee's kids while she and Tyler went out."

"Tyler?" she asked.

"Yeah, why do you sound so surprised?"

"I'm not... I mean... I know they were having trouble."

"Yeah, that's one of the reasons why I agreed to watch the kids. They need this time together."

"Yeah. I just thought Tyler was doing something else, that's all."

"How do you know?"

"I talked to him earlier and he said he had to do something for his parents. Liar."

"Okay what's going on with y'all," I asked facing her.

"Why do you think something is going on?"

"First you were surprised Sherri was with Tyler, and you are too concerned about him lying to you."

"Sherri and I have been friends forever and I would never do anything to hurt her."

"So what's the problem?"

Kina grunted and leaned forward, placing her head in her hands. She looked back up at me.

"I need to tell you something, but promise me you want say anything until I sort this out. I haven't even said anything to Alexis about it."

"Okay...." I replied anxious for her to get on with it.

"Tyler and I have been talking on the phone, he wants to keep seeing each other and I don't know what to do," she blurted out.

"You gotta be kidding me," I said getting up from the chair.

I headed into the kitchen to get away. I wasn't sure if I wanted away from her or the news. While there I began to make myself a drink. I grabbed a glass from the cabinet and got some ice. I poured some Pepsi in my glass and realized I needed something a little stronger. I went to get the key to the alcohol case and grabbed out a half-empty bottle of Hennessey. I poured a little in my glass and Kina walked into the kitchen.

"I didn't mean for it to happen. I..."

She opened her mouth to speak but I help up my hand to stop her. I took a swig of the drink to make room for some more Hennessey. I finally turned around to face her.

"I don't want to hear it. I can't believe this," I said walking out of the kitchen.

"I'm so sorry," she said right behind my heels.

"Don't be sorry for me," I replied taking another swallow of my drink. "What do you mean you don't know what to do? That's obvious. How did all of this start?" I asked noticing she had the bottle in her hand. She poured herself a shot before she answered.

"We ran into each other at the grocery store."

"And..."

"And he was stressing over an exam. He hadn't really studied so I offered him a plate and we've been talking on the phone."

"Were you planning on hooking up when you made the offer?"

"No, of course not."

"How does something like this just happen?"

"I mean I was feeling down about what is going on with Micah. Most of our sorority sisters are married or in a relationship and I still can't find a decent man. I've been stressed out wondering if something is wrong with me, going on diets and stuff. So when he complimented me, I was... flattered."

I sat there silent. I couldn't think of anything to say to her. While I watched at her in disbelief, I heard someone at the door. Once at the door, I looked through the peephole to see Stephanie and J.B.

"Hey girl, is everything all right?" I asked.

On her way through the door I could see that her eyes were puffy and red. She was holding J.B., who was fast asleep.

"No. I had another argument with Brad... I'm sorry I didn't know you had company," she replied noticing Kina now standing.

"It's cool; I'm going to head out. Tammy I'll call you later," Kina stated as she quickly left.

"You better," I said as I closed the door behind her. Sensing that it was going to be a while with Stephanie, I went a made myself a refill of Pepsi. Somehow I managed to become the resident therapist.

"You can lay him down in Rod's room next to Derrick," I said to Stephanie noticing her struggling to hold him up.

"Thanks," she said barely making eye contact.

I went into Janise's room to check on the girls. They were tucked away peacefully and for a moment I envied their solace. I took a swig of my drink and went back up front with Stephanie.

"You want something to drink?" I asked her as I reentered the living room.

"No thanks."

"So, what's up?" I inquired as I took a seat beside her.

"You know I was supposed to be trying to smooth this whole situation over with Brad this weekend," she reviewed the details her voice cracking.

"Yeah, I remember."

"Anyway, when I brought it up he didn't even want to discuss it. But Jonathan keeps insisting that I let him see J.B. I suggested that we meet somewhere neutral but I wasn't going to tell J.B. that he was his father," she continued. The more she went on the stronger her voice became.

"Did he agree to it?"

"Yeah, Jonathan understands that this is all new for J.B. and that a relationship with him is going to take time."

"Well, what's the problem?"

"Somehow Brad found out that we met him at Putt Putt. He went off about me going behind his back and he thinks I might be cheating on him."

"He should have known it was for your son, but why didn't you tell him that you were meeting him?"

"Because I know how he can be, I was going to tell him after the fact. It's not like I was hiding it."

"Yeah, well withholding information could seem suspect, especially in a new relationship."

"I admit that, but the bulk of the argument is about Jonathan getting to know his son. He said that Jonathan is stupid if he thinks that he's going to roll in 8 years late. We had a huge fight about it and he kicked us out," she explained and finally dropped a few tears.

"Oh no. He didn't hurt you did he," I asked while pulling her into an embrace.

"No, I'm fine."

"Where are you staying?" I asked pulling back to look her in the face.

"At my mom's... again. It's just until I get a new apartment."

"Well you know I'm here for you if you need anything."

"I know. You always are. This time I'm going to get it together myself. Things would be so much easier if Jonathan would have stayed gone."

Alexis

The attacker had a tight grip on my mouth and I could barely breathe through my nose. As he held me I couldn't help but wonder if this was it for me.

"You know; at first I thought I found your brother when I saw A. Moretti on the mailbox back in Greensboro. Imagine my surprise when I found out it was his baby sister. You thought you were slick moving to Winston, huh?"

Finally, he released me from his grip taking my phone from me. I rushed to the other side of my apartment.

He was about 6 foot 3, chocolate complexion. Something about him was familiar but I couldn't see his face well because of his hoodie. I attempted to make a run for it but another male came from the back carrying my laptop.

"I wouldn't do that if I were you," he said as he made his way toward me aiming his gun. He had on a hoodie too but his cold eyes were staring right at me and the image was stuck in my head.

"I'm sure my friend has called the police by now," I lied hoping that it was true.

"Calm down, our beef is with your brother this time. We just came to get a down payment. You be sure to tell him that unless I get another 5 g's; I'll be back over here."

After they left I just stood there in shock for a few minutes unable to process what had happened. What did he mean this time? I kept trying to place the guy with the hoodie. I pushed back the feeling that the past was coming back to haunt me and then realized that I should lock the door in case they change their minds and came back. Unfortunately the lock was broken. Just as I was struggling with it I heard someone pound on the door. With tears in my eyes I fought to keep the door close long enough to hook the latch.

"It's me, open up," I heard Missy yell.

Relieved it was only her, I stopped struggling.

"I rushed over here when you didn't answer your phone ... What happened?!" she asked noticing the house and my fragile state.

"There were two guys in here when I got home...," I answered pacing the floor trying to recap everything, "they said something about Lex owing some money... it all happened so fast."

"Oh, my god! Are you okay?"

"I'm fine, but they got my laptop, my cell, and who knows what else, I haven't looked to see what all is missing. Let me see your phone so I can call the police," I directed walking towards her.

"Wait," she replied holding her hand up to stop me, "I already called Lex on my way over here. I figured you might be in trouble."

"I need to file a report, they got my laptop and who knows if they will come back or not" I said almost in tears.

"Just calm down. They said he owes them some money; just give him a chance to get your stuff back first."

"Fine," I said throwing my hand up in compliance. I hooked the latch back on the door then went to see what all was missing. My clothes were sprawled all over my bedroom and I noticed the flat screen was gone. I heard several cars pull up outside so I peeked out the window to see what was going on. There were three SUV's outside and about ten guys jumped out of the trucks. I paced the floor of my room hoping that it wasn't another surprise attack. Frantically, I searched my room for something I could use as a weapon. I bent down to grab my stiletto off the floor and the crash of the door being kicked in froze me.

"Where my sister at?" Lex yelled.

Still angry with him, I ran up front and threw a couple blows at his chest. He pulled me into his arms and I gave up and rested in his embrace. For a moment I felt secure. He let me go and wiped the tears from my eyes and I thought I saw a couple in his.

"What happened," he asked his face growing stiff.

"When I got home the door was open and these dudes were in the house. They grabbed me and took my phone and some other stuff."

"What else?" an older guy asked.

"They said that they want another 5 g's and if you didn't pay they would be back," I said still focused on Lex, my voice cracking on the last words.

Before I could finish talking Lex punched the wall beside him leaving an imprint of his anger. He walked outside for a minute.

"What did they look like," J.O. asked.

"Yeah, what they have on," another one added.

"They had on hoodies and one of them had a bandana on his face."

"What color," J.O. asked.

"Don't even trip, I know who it is," Lex said coming back into the apartment. "Come on, y'all, let's roll."

"I hope you aren't going to do anything stupid, I could just call the police," I said stopping him.

"Man, hell nah. I'm gone handle this. You just go over Missy's house tonight and I'll call you later."

"Just be careful," I called out to his back because he and his squad were almost in the jeep.

"I can meet you at your house if you want to go," I said turning to Missy.

"Girl bye, I'm not leaving you here by yourself."

I gathered a couple outfits from the mess in my room and threw them in an overnight bag.

Sherri

After dinner with Tyler I couldn't sleep. All I could think about is what he neglected to tell me and the discouraged look he had when I said I might have the kids. I know all too well that Tyler doesn't want any kids in his life right now and I wondered if my sister's disappearing act was threatening my relationship. Even though I didn't get any rest, I went ahead and got the kids from Tammy's around 9 the next morning.

"Hey girl, we were just finishing up breakfast. You didn't have to rush."

"That's okay. You've been a big help. I hate you had to give up you kid free weekend."

"Don't even sweat it. I'm here for you whenever."

"You guys go get your stuff together," I said to the kids who were intently focused on the cartoons. "So what did y'all do last night," I asked Tammy as I waited for the kids.

"Not much. The kids were asleep by ten. Stephanie came over for a while and we talked."

"How's she doing?"

"She'll be fine; man trouble."

"You can say that again. Seeing Tyler wasn't the break that I wasn't looking for."

"Hmm," Tammy replied and was interrupted by the kids bursting into the room. "I enjoyed you guys, y'all come back and visit."

"We will," Terra replied.

"I'm gone; call me later," I said as I hugged her. I grabbed Derrick up and got his diaper bag off the table.

"Wait a second," Tammy said before I could leave and walked closer to me.

"Girls, go ahead in get in the car," I told them noticing the seriousness in Tammy's expression.

"Everything okay," I asked.

"Yeah," she answered trying to lighten her demeanor but I could still see the worry lines. "I just wanted to say be sure you talk to Kina. She's going through something and you two should talk."

"Okay," I replied a bit confused, "so that's all that you will tell me. You know I don't do well with anticipation."

"Just trust me; you should talk to her yourself."

"Okay," I conceded, realizing she wasn't going to say anything. I gave her a hug and went to meet the girls in the car.

"You talked to Mommy yet?" Michelle asked as I was fastening Derrick into his car seat.

"Uh, not yet."

"Where we going?" Terra asked.

"We are going over Nana's house for a little while."

"Okay," she said, satisfied with the response.

I turned on the radio hoping that the children wouldn't ask anymore questions. I never know what to say to them; I don't want them to worry anymore than they have to. I pulled up to my mom's house and Terra and Michelle were out the car before it stopped.

"Hey babies," my mom said as she came outside. I got Derrick and his things out of the car.

"Hey ma," I said reaching to give her a hug, instead she grabbed Derrick.

"Hey baby," she answered me. "Y'all had breakfast yet," she asked the kids.

I walked in to the house and went upstairs to what used to be my room. I sat down for a moment on my bed and looked at the pictures that still decorated my dresser mirror. I saw one with me, Kina, and Tyler at WSSU. I thought about how fun and carefree we were then. Below it was a more recent picture of Tyler at Wake Forest University. I walked over to pick it up.

"How is Tyler? He hasn't been over in a while," my mom asked now standing in the doorway.

"He's been pretty busy at school."

"You know, Monica and I almost died when we found out y'all were dating," she said giving off a light chuckle. "Now all we are waiting for is the engagement announcement," she said with a proud grin.

"I don't know about that Mama," I admitted feeling my eyes water but I held back.

"What do you mean? You and Tyler get along great with each other. I know we gave you a hard time at first but you two should get married," she said as she came further into the room and sat down next to me on the bed.

"Yeah, well we might not be together much longer."

"What's going on?" she asked.

"I don't know. I really don't want to talk about it," I answered and lay back onto my bed.

"Okay, but your father and I are always here. Your room may be full but our arms are always open," she said slowly getting up from the bed.

"I know."

I jumped up off the bed and the clock read 12:15; I realized I must have fallen asleep. I walked downstairs to see where everyone was.

"Hey sleepyhead," my dad greeted me from the living room.

"Why didn't anybody wake me up?" I asked as I took seat beside him.

"You looked like you could use some rest." He put his arm around me and gave me a peck on the forehead.

"Where are Mom and the kids?"

"They went to the grocery store to get something for dinner."

"I need to go home and do some laundry; tell ma I'll be back to pick them up."

"For what? They'll be fine."

"Okay. I'll still be back for dinner."

When I got home I saw Tommy's Lincoln in the parking lot. I didn't see him in the car so I headed up to my apartment. He was headed down the stairs as I was coming up. His eye was swollen and his face covered with bruises; the only reason I recognized him so quickly was because of his chain.

"Yo, where my kids at?" he asked.

"Why? You do not need to see them looking like that, what happened to you?"

"Never mind that, I been trying to reach you all weekend. I heard Renee is missing. Those are my girls; they need to be with their father."

"They are fine where they are," I said, my worst fear coming true, "besides do you really think that it would do them any good to see you like this?"

He paused for a moment and I hoped that I had convinced him.

"Look, I know you are trying to look out for them but believe that I'm going to get my girls."

He turned to go back to his car. Seeing him like that made me wonder if he had anything to do with my sister's disappearance. I made a mental note to talk to my boss about what legal rights we have when it comes to the girls. I went inside and started my laundry. After the conversation with my mom I realized that Tyler needed to make a decision. I'm tired of stressing day by day because we are standing on thin ice. I called his apartment but I didn't recognize the voice on the line.

"Is Tyler there?"

"No he is on campus, may I ask who's calling?"

"This is Sherri," I answered. I wondered if he had girls calling him often.

"Oh, hi Sherri. This is Jaleel. Tyler talks about you all the time. I'll definitely let him know you called."

"Thanks."

I hung up the phone glad to hear that he at least talks about me. I just hope it was a favorable conversation.

Alexis

I was startled awake by a car door slamming. It took me a minute to get my bearings. Nothing looked familiar and after a minute I remembered that I was at Missy's house awkwardly lying across her sofa. Missy passed through the living room and bid me good morning before she walked out the door. Scenes from last night kept replaying in my head. The attacker in the hoodie kept flashing in my mind and haunted me because I couldn't place him. There was something about him that I remembered and I couldn't let it go. I heard arguing outside so I peeked out the window. Missy was arguing with some guy. His back was to me so I couldn't see his face. He was wearing a throwback jersey with the matching hat and sneakers. I went to grab the house phone just in case I had to call the police. Before I could find the phone I heard the car speed off and Missy walked in the door.

"Everything okay?" I asked her.

"I'm fine. That was K.D. coming over here tripping about me blowing up at his house and I am not trying to hear it. He should have thought about that before he started sleeping around. Please, I do not have time for that."

"So, you're straight?" I asked as I picked up the cover I was using to put it up.

"Yeah," Missy answered and grabbed the blanket from me.

"I'm leaving for work early," I called to her down the hall, "I need to stop by my apartment to grab some things."

"You going by yourself?" she asked from the end of the hallway

"Yeah, I'm fine. Besides I'm just running in for a minute."

The stop home made me about five minutes late. I rushed to get my shift started and I didn't notice that Eugene was at the store.

"I'm surprised to see you here," I commented.

"Hey, I'm sorry about last night," he came over to give me a hug.

"It's cool," I said savoring the moment in his arms. After the commotion of everything it felt good to be there.

"Is everything okay," he asked letting me go. "I called you a couple times and when you didn't call back I was worried you were still mad about me canceling."

"No, I lost my phone," I alleged not wanting to say what really happened.

"Good. I mean…not about the phone."

"I figured, so when are you going to make it up?"

"I was hoping you could come over tonight. My buddy, Lance, is still here but I want you to be there."

"That sounds good. Are you buying anything while you are here?"

"No, I just came to see that lovely smile."

"Okay," I said blushing. "I hope you can cook."

"I can throw down."

"All right, I'll see you tonight."

After Eugene left Jerry approached me with an excited look on his face that told me we must have received a good report from Bridgette.

"I have some good news for you... Bridgette called earlier to say that our department was highest in productivity and guess who she was most impressed with... Ms. Alexis Moretti! She's thinking of promoting you; you need to call and set up a meeting."

"Oh my gosh, that's amazing," I said faking enthusiasm. I'm glad that she took notice of me, but I realized that a promotion would take even more of my limited time.

"Congratulations. Let's do dinner after work to celebrate."

"I don't think that is a good idea."

"C'mon it'll be fun. It's just dinner, strictly professional"

"I already have plans. Besides, I don't feel comfortable with that..."

"With what..." while he was talking my brother came in. Glad for the exit I went to greet him. He had my laptop in hand.

"I told you I would take care of it. Oh, here is your phone," he reached in his pocket and handed my iPhone.

"Thanks," was all I said. I knew better than to ask any questions.

"Well it is all taken care of now; you don't have to worry about them anymore. I put the rest of your stuff back at the apartment and we got a new lock on until we find you a new place…So who is that you were talking to over there?" he asked peering over my shoulder at Jerry.

"Nobody, just the manager."

"Is everything all right? You seem a little tense. Is that the Jerry dude that keeps asking you out?" he asked grilling in Jerry's direction.

"Nah, it's nothing I was just a little late for work," I lied.

"All right, well call me later."

After work, I went out to my car and noticed an envelope in my windshield wiper. Reluctantly, I picked it up. I was relieved to see it was addressed to Lexie Pie, a nickname Isaiah gave me despite my objections. Without opening it, I put the letter in my purse so that I could get ready for my date with Eugene.

Detective Myers

I sat at my desk looking over the case files that Captain Discher left for me. A missing woman case caught my eye. The lady had been missing for almost two weeks.

"Hey Myers, you had a chance to look at that Robinson case?" Officer Jenkins asked coming over to my desk.

"I'm looking at it now, what's up?"

"The sister called again today; she's having a problem with the father of the girls. She wants to talk with someone; you want me to send Graves over to talk with her?"

"No, I'll handle it," I responded as I flipped through the case file. Tommy had already raised a few eyebrows. After talking with Sherri on the phone, I made a note to go question him, but first we had a lead on the Cadillac that Renee's co-worker, Helen, described. After reviewing the surveillance tapes from the restaurant, we got the plates of the vehicle and found out that it was registered to Kenneth James. He had a record of assault on a female. He was charged with assault and battery and served a year in prison. He was picked up a couple of months ago during a sting operation of a small time gang on the north side of town. The case was thrown out because evidence leading to the sting was linked to a dirty undercover detective and some other technical errors during the arrests. Looking at his history I decided to bring him in for questioning.

"What is this about detective, I need to be at work," Kenneth said reclining in the chair.

"I see you were picked up in July during a drug bust at the park."

"I know that's not what this is about. Those charges were dropped, this is going on harassment"

"Yeah, but you were found guilty for assault and battery."

"That's ancient history, besides I did my time."

"Yeah but it looks like you are up to your old tricks."

"Man, what are you talking about?" he asked no longer so cocky.

"I'm talking about your girlfriend, Renee Robinson?"

"I don't know anybody by that name," he said straightening himself in the chair making me doubt his response.

"Really? Her co-worker saw her leave with you Thursday March 2nd and now she's missing."

"Whoa, you got the wrong guy. I didn't have anything to do with that."

"Really, I'm thinking you did have something to do with it. What happened Kenneth? Did she threaten to break things off?"

"Like I said, I don't know her."

"Okay. But if we find out you did something to Renee, prison time is the least of your worries."

After the interrogation one of the officers came in with the background check on Tommy Peterson, the father of the two oldest children. Tommy had a misdemeanor drug charge a couple of years ago. He's known to be affiliated with a gang called the Rack Squad which happened to be rivals with the people Kenny was affiliated with. I decided to mention it to Tommy to see if Kenny was lying about knowing Renee. My partner, Eric, and I went to check out the address we had on record for him in High Point with no luck. Next we went to a known territory of the Rack Squad. We found Tommy curbside and he made us quick. He attempted to run but Eric cut him off. We found a couple of grams of coke on him so we used it as leeway to get information on Renee back at the interrogation room.

"I want a lawyer," he exclaimed not long after he was seated.

"Relax, he is on the way. Besides, I'm not from the narcotics unit. I'm here about Renee, you know it's a shame what happened to her."

"Whatever happened to her aint have nothing to do with me," he insisted then folded his arms and sat back in the chair.

"Is that right? The way I see it, she gets a new boyfriend and you get a little jealous, so you rough her up a little bit, teach her a lesson."

"Look, me and Renee broke up a long time ago, I could care less who she is with."

"Really, it didn't tick you off that her new boyfriend was in a rival gang?"

"Look, I been known her last baby daddy rolled with them; she did that mess to get back at me. Besides she made herself look stupid messing with a married man. He ain't even about the gangsta life."

"Maybe he found out about you," I continued not wanting to let on that I didn't know that Kenneth was the younger child's father. "What happened to your face? Did he come and tighten you up?"

"Look, I aint saying nothing else until my lawyer gets here."

I realized I wasn't going to get anything else out of him. It was clear that Kenneth was lying; not only that, it looks like he could be the father of 2 year old Derrick. That made me wonder if she threatened to come out about their son and he went after her or if we have a jealous wife on our hands.

Chapter 6

Kina

I hadn't been able to concentrate on my work. I can't believe I let things get this far between Tyler and me. He told me that he is breaking up with Sherri after everything blows over with her sister but that doesn't make me feel any better, worse actually. He has been calling my phone but I can't bring myself to answer it. I finished the article on the convenience store robbery that the editor has been sweating me over but I've been looking at my screensaver since then. The pink and green Omega Psi Phi banner going across almost brought me to tears. I could hear our line captain yelling what those letters meant to us.

"Friendship is essential to the soul! When you leave this university, not only will you have an education, you will have sisters. Ladies give me the step!"

"Omega…Psi…Phiii!" we yelled in unison then began rhythmically stomping and clapping our hands.

"Hey girl," Alexis said as she entered my office bringing me back to the present.

"Hey Alexis. When did you get here?"

"I just walked in. You won't believe what happened to me," she confided as she took a seat across from my desk.

"What?"

"You remember those notes I told you about?" She paused long enough for me to nod in agreement than continued rambling.

"Well, after I dropped you off I went home. There were these guys in my house, and they took some things, and said that if Lex didn't pay them they would be back."

"Oh my gosh," I said in an outburst then lowered my voice once I remembered where we were. "Are you okay?"

"I'm fine. Lex brought me my stuff at Glam and fixed my lock."

"Did he pay them?"

"I didn't ask him any questions. I just hope that it's all over."

"That is crazy. Do you want to stay at my place for a while?"

"I should be fine. Hopefully it's all over."

"That's what we thought the last time. Do you think that this has anything to do with what happened in college?" I asked convinced that this had something to do with the drug deal Alexis got caught up in back then.

"I'm not so sure anymore. Lex said that he had everything under control but something the attacker said threw me off. He said that he wasn't after me this time."

"Maybe you should go to the police." I suggested.

"You know I can't do that. Besides I don't know how much my brother has done to keep me out of trouble. I would hate for him to get caught up for my screw-up."

"Did you recognize the guy who attacked you?"

"There were three. I don't know any of them but one guy seemed familiar."

"Was he someone that hung out with Dante?" I asked wondering if he was an associate of Alexis' ex-boyfriend who got her in trouble in college.

"I don't think so; it's like I have seen him somewhere else."

"Maybe you should stay with me for a while, at least until all this blows over."

"You sure," she asked.

"Of course," I replied, "besides I can use the company."

"How are you doing with the break up?" she asked.

"Not too good…"

"Trust me; Micah is not worth the hassle."

"It's not him… I gotta tell you something but don't say anything to the girls."

"Okay, what's up?"

"I've been seeing somebody else."

"So what's the problem?"

"He's in a relationship," I revealed and her draw dropped. "We've been talking and we hooked up once but…"

"Did you know he had a girl when y'all hooked up?"

"That's what's got me messed up. I was too busy feeling sorry for myself that when he was attracted to me I didn't think about how it would affect his girlfriend. Now I feel so stupid," I said and finally let go of the tears I'd been holding.

"Oh, Kina..." she said taking hold of my arm. "You still seeing him?"

"I haven't talked to him since, but I don't want to. I wish I could take it back," I answered as I wiped my face with the Kleenex on my desk. My phone rang again and I saw it was Tyler calling again. "He's calling now," I told her.

"Just let him now it's over and try to put this behind you. I'm here if you need me," she said then left my office.

I answered the phone but couldn't bring myself to say anything.

"Hello…" Tyler eventually said.

"Hey…before you say anything, I don't think we should keep seeing each other."

"I understand. Are you going to tell Sherri about this?"

"Should I?"

"It's up to you. I told you I'm ending things regardless."

"I just want to put all this behind me."

"You didn't tell anyone did you?"

"No."

"Then, don't worry about it. Sherri's got enough to deal with. I guess this is good bye."

"Yeah," I agreed and hung up. I attempted to do some research then I remembered my drunken revelation at Tammy's house. I know I was a little tipsy but I couldn't believe I told her. I sat at my desk and unsuccessfully tried to recall all that I mentioned to her. Thanks to the three Bud lights I drank before I got there I couldn't remember what I told her. I needed to call and feel her out.

"Hey Tammy," I said as she answered her cell.

"You didn't have to work today?" she asked.

"I'm on lunch. Can you talk?"

"Yeah, I'm at home."

"I talked to Tyler and let him know that we shouldn't talk to each other anymore."

"Good, but you still should be up front with Sherri."

"She just has so much to deal with right now; I don't see the point of adding to it."

"Wouldn't you want to know?"

"I don't know," I said honestly. "Have you said anything to her?"

"That's not my place, but I still think you should tell her."

"Maybe when this thing with her sister is over. How do you think she will take it, I mean is it as bad as it sounds?"

"Worse," she replied.

"You don't think she will end our friendship, I mean we've been friends since we pledged freshman year."

"Honestly, I don't know," she responded.

"Maybe we shouldn't tell her. Tyler is not worth losing what we have."

Alexis

Eugene's place was beautiful. It was a two bedroom, two bathroom house. He had an African theme going and it was tastefully decorated. If I didn't know any better I would have thought a woman was responsible. I checked every photo to be sure.

"It's nice to finally meet you. G' talks about you all the time," Lance said shaking my hand.

"All good I hope."

"Some of it," he replied playfully.

"It smells delicious in here. Where is the chef?" I asked.

"At your service," he said coming out wearing an apron.

"Wow, its Chef Hood-ar-G'," his friend joked.

"You know it. Dinner will be ready in about fifteen minutes; can I fix you something to drink?"

"What do you have?" I asked.

"Just about everything," he said showing me his selection at the bar counter.

"I'll have some white wine."

"Let me get a beer," Lance asked.

"You know where they are."

"Are you two always like this?" I asked.

"No, he's just showing out in front of company," Lance answered after grabbing his Bud Ice from the mini fridge.

"Actually, this is a little mild. I already told Lance to be on his best behavior. I would hate to scare you off," Eugene answered as he handed me my glass.

"Please, you can't be any worse than my brother and his friends."

"You two close?" Eugene inquired.

"We're working on it. We grew up separately."

"Well, you can have a seat in the dining room. Dinner will be out in just a moment."

I noticed Isaiah's letter peeking out of my bag. Unsure of its contents I pushed it down before it fell out.

"Do you want me to put up your purse?"

"Sure," I answered hesitantly.

He took my things and sat them in what looked like a guest room. Eugene served a southern meal: fried chicken, baked macaroni, greens.

"I have to hand it to you, you can cook," I said finishing my plate.

"I taught him everything he knows," Lance commented.

"Yeah, I learned everything there is to know about oodles of noodles and grilled cheese from you."

"This is my last night in town. We have to finish with a bang. Can we get a refill on these drinks, G'."

"Coming up."

We all headed back into the sitting area.

"Alexis, Truth or Dare?" Lance asked me.

"You don't have to answer that," Eugene replied.

"It's okay," I answered, "truth."

"All right…Are you going to give G' the cookies since he cooked for you?"

"Wow…not yet?"

"Ahh! But she said yet G' you almost in there."

"You are too much," I replied shaking my head, my cheeks blushing with embarrassment. Despite these childish antics I still couldn't convince myself to leave.

Eugene walked over with the drinks.

"Your turn G' truth or dare?"

"Truth…" he answered looking sternly at Lance.

"How did you get that scar on your leg?"

"You already know how I got it."

"Just answer the question."

"I fell my sophomore year at WSSU."

"How did you fall?" I asked sensing there was more to the story.

"Yeah, G', how did you fall?" Lance asked and dramatically turned towards Eugene as if it was his first time hearing the story.

"Okay, okay. We were streaking Blair Hall and I got distracted and ran into a bench."

"You should have seen him, he did a 360 around the bench," Lance added bursting into laughter.

"All right, since you have such a good memory," he said turning to Lance, "I'm sure Alexis would like to hear about your accident on the four wheeler at the beach."

"It aint my turn."

"Yes it is, truth or dare," Eugene continued.

"Dare."

"Okay, you want to switch it up… I dare you to go outside and sing Kelis' 'Milkshake' as loud as you can, no coat."

"I'm a thug baby, it aint nothing."

After a few moments we could hear him outside.

"You guys are crazy," I commented.

"Yeah, I know. I wanted to be alone for a moment anyway."

"Is that right."

He leaned over and planted a kiss on my lips that sent a warm sensation through my veins. Lance walked in right as I was hitting Mars and brought me back down to Earth.

"It's getting late you guys, I better get going," I said clumsily stumbling past the chair.

"Leaving so soon? We were just starting to have fun," Lance insisted.

"I wish I could stay, but I have an early meeting tomorrow at Glam."

"I'll walk you to your car," Eugene offered before excusing himself to gather my things.

"It was nice meeting you Alexis," said Lance as he extended his hand.

"Yes, this was…interesting," I replied accepting his handshake. Eugene reentered with my purse and gently took a hold of my hand. Our connection intensified by the brief contact of our mingling fingers. I followed his lead to my car, my heart racing. Being with Eugene brought back feelings I hadn't felt in years; feelings I tried hard to forget. Memories made me quickly release his hand.

"Everything okay?" he asked.

"Yes," I answered as I pulled my keys from my purse, "Thank you again for having me over."

"Really, you aren't too freaked out are you; Lance can get a little crazy sometimes."

"I admit I was thrown off by the Truth or Dare but I think you guys are hilarious."

"So when can I see you again?" he asked facing me his eyes sparkling with a grin decorated by his dimples.

'Tomorrow,' I thought but I suppressed the enthusiasm, "I'm not sure, I've been busy lately with work and the internship. Just call me."

I sat down in the car before he could enter my personal space again.

"I will," he replied.

I wove goodbye as I drove away. At home mixed emotions overwhelmed me. I foolishly convinced myself that Eugene and I could just be friends but after tonight the truth was obvious. I had to end this immediately.

Even with the new locks and security system combined with Lex's assurance that the situation was over, I was still a little uneasy being alone in my apartment. I grabbed some clothes and supplies to take with me to Kina's once I got off work. My evaluation with the owner at Glam went well. She unofficially assured me that I would be promoted to manager. Even though I'm more interested in my writing career I was still buzzing off the good news when I started work and I couldn't wait to tell Missy.

"Congratulations, even though we all know how you got the job," she said indifferently.

"Excuse me," I said shocked by her accusation.

"Here we go with the school girl routine. Don't front like you don't know the only reason why you was even considered was because of Jerry boosting you up because he's trying to get with you."

"Whatever, even if he 'boosted it up', if Bridgette didn't agree she wouldn't have asked me for the interview. And that I passed on my own so don't try and hate on me because you are jealous that I got the promotion and you didn't."

"Jealous, girl please! I'm about to get back to work before I say something I might regret."

That was the best idea she had all day because I could think of a few things I would like to say to her. I couldn't believe that she of all people was sleeping on my promotion.

Back at Kina's apartment I was excited about my promotion but conflicted about how Missy flipped on me. I started to call Eugene and tell him the good news but I remembered he had to work tonight. I listened to my messages and heard one from Isaiah asking me to call him back. I went to my purse to read his letter and couldn't find it. I thought about the incident and Eugene's house and wondered if it fell out. I thought about calling him about it but then he would want to know who it was from. I checked the clock to see if Kina was off yet.

"Hey girl, what's up," she answered her phone.

"Not much, how are you doing?"

"I'm good. You remember Isaiah, right?"

"Yeah…"

"Well he gave me a letter a work and I think I left it at Eugene's house."

"Why would you even have it there?"

"It was in my purse and I think it might have fallen out. I don't even know what it says yet."

"Did you call Eugene to see if he found it?"

"Imagine that conversation. 'Hey, did you find an envelope addressed Lexie Pie; my ex' gave it to me and I need it back."

"Maybe you left it somewhere else. Are you sure you lost it there?"

"It was the last place I remember having it. Maybe I should invite myself over again and look for it."

"Just don't say anything about it. He may not find it and if he does you can play cool. It wasn't opened right? You could say it was from your brother."

"I guess."

"I gotta go; I'm finishing this article. We can talk when I get home."

I liked her plan but I couldn't risk him finding it. At the same time there wasn't much I could do about it. I headed over to my brother's house to get my lie straight.

"I just got her to sleep; please don't wake her up," Trina begged as I walked over to the bassinet.

"I won't. I just want to look at her. She is too cute." I walked back to where Trina was, "How are you doing?"

"I'm good but I'm ready to get back in the studio. Would you mind baby-sitting while I record sometime?"

"You know I don't mind looking after Lexie but don't you think it's too soon to be back at work?"

"Not really; it's not like I have to do any physical labor. Besides, I'm bout to go crazy being shut up in the house all the time."

"Well I'll watch her whenever I can. Is Lex around? I need to ask him something."

"He's at work. Is everything o.k.?"

"Yeah. I lost a letter I got from my ex' at Eugene's house and if he finds it I'm going to say it's from him."

"Why don't you go back over and find it before he does?"

"I thought about that. He's at work now though. I just want a back-up plan."

"Shoot, you ought to go now while he is gone."

"I would if I had a key but we've had like two dates."

"You don't need a key, just a credit card."

"Are you serious?"

"As a heart attack."

Lex and his friends walked in.

"What's good," he greeted us.

"Not much, I was just talking with Alexis about going back to work."

"For what; it's not like we need the money. I don't want my baby going to daycare or stuck with some nanny."

"Well between Missy and Alexis we won't need one."

"We'll talk about it later. What's been up with you, Baby Sis? Everything cool at work?"

"Yup. I start training next week and I should be promoted in the next couple of months."

"That's what's up," Lex said.

"Lex, can you stay here with the baby for a minute," Trina asked, "I'm going to ride to the store with Alexis to get out the house for a while."

"Okay but hurry back," he answered.

"You sure you want to go," I asked her trying to talk her out of this ridiculous plan.

"Definitely," she said grabbing her purse and heading out the door.

Tammy

I was headed out the door to visit Sherri and two police officers were headed up my front porch.

"Mrs. James, I'm Detective Myers. We just have a couple questions for you."

"Actually, I'm on my way out," I said locking my door, "What's this about?"

"A young lady named Renee Robinson, do you know her?"

"Yes, but you knew that already or else you wouldn't be here," I replied shifting my purse securely on my shoulder.

"We just want to see what you know about her disappearance."

"I really don't know anything but what Sherri has told me."

"Were you aware that Kenneth was in a relationship with her?"

"No I wasn't…Did he have something to do with this?"

"I don't know. Did you know that he could be the father of her son?"

"Her son…He's two, I mean we were still…"

"Right, you were still married. Did she confront you about it? Maybe you two got into it…"

"No, this is the first I've heard about it. Even if I had known I wouldn't have done anything to her…Do I need a lawyer?"

"I don't know. When was the last time you saw Renee?"

"Look, I'm not answering anymore questions. If you aren't charging me with anything then you can leave."

I could not believe that Kenny was Derrick's father or that I'm even being considered as a suspect in Renee's disappearance. I love Sherri like a sister; I could never do anything to hurt her or her sister. I started to call Kenny about the whole thing but I dropped it since the kids were still there and I don't want them to know anything about it yet. On my way to the car I got a call from Stephanie.

"Hey girl, guess what?" she sang excitedly.

"What's up?" I said not open for conversation at the moment.

"Me and Brad made up again and he let me and J.B. move back in."

"Really? So, he's cool with Jonathan seeing J.B.?"

"Well he said that he's sorry about the fight and that he wants to work it out."

"What did J.B. think about meeting Jonathan?"

"He thought he was cool, but he doesn't understand why he has to hang with him. I think we are going to have to tell him Jonathan's his father."

"What does Brad think about that?"

"I haven't brought it up yet, but Jonathan thinks that it's long overdue so I'll talk to him about it tonight."

"Well I have to go; let me know how it goes."

Detective Myers

After talking with Kenneth's wife, I'm positive that she didn't have anything to do with Renee's disappearance. I could tell that the first she heard about the affair is when I told her. Today is supposed to be my day off but I decided to go by Renee's house again. There has to be something we missed; something that could tell us what she was into before she went missing. When I went through her bedroom I found a card key to Holiday Inn. I tracked it down to the one in Winston-Salem. I called Eric to meet me there. I showed the receptionist a photo of Renee and he didn't recognize her. I had him check the records to see if any room was charged in her name and he said no. Then I had him try Kenneth James. The hotel records showed that he had a room there Thursday, March 2nd and he checked out that Friday which was around the time Renee went missing. We checked with the rest of the staff that worked that night to see if any of them remembered seeing Renee that night. Finally, we talked with one of the attendants who remembered seeing her.
"Yeah, I remember her being here."
"Are you sure it was her."
"Positive. I was on my way to the elevator to take up an order; she was leaving in a hurry and almost knocked my trays over."

"Was anyone with her?"

"No, she was by herself."

Next we checked with security to see if we could review the tapes for that night. We tracked her as far as the parking lot leaving on foot. I called detective Timothy Harris, an old friend of mine, at the Winston-Salem Police Department to see if they had any calls that night involving a woman matching her description.

"I had Officer Keiser check with dispatch and someone called in to report a woman found on Mystic Drive not too far from the hotel."

"Where is she now?"

"EMS took her to Baptist Hospital. If I'm not mistaken she's still there under Jane Doe. We started an investigation but the trail went cold."

"Thanks Tim, I think that may be my girl."

Sherri

I dropped the kids off at mama's house and when I got back to the car I realized I left my phone in the seat. I saw that I had a voicemail from Detective Myers; she said that they had a lead and that I should come to the station as soon as possible. I arrived at the station and one of the officers had me wait for what seemed like forever before detective Myers came out. Her facial expression showed that whatever news she had was not good.
"I came as soon as I got your message."
"Ms. Robinson, we think we may have found your sister at Baptist. We didn't come across her at first because she was registered as a Jane Doe. Somebody saw her lying beside the road and called it in."
"Oh my God! Is she still alive?"
"Yes, but she is in the ICU with a coma; I need you to ride with me to the hospital so that we can get a positive I.D."
 I called Tammy to see if she would watch the kids but I got her voicemail. I tried Alexis and thankfully she was available. When we went to identify Renee I could hardly recognize her because she was beaten so badly. She arrived at the hospital that Thursday, March 2nd and she has been comatose since. Her head was shaved

and bandaged and a monitor was hooked to her head. Her doctor, Patricia Waters, came in to meet us.

"Are those machines keeping her alive?" I asked

"No they are monitoring her intracranial pressure and brain activity."

"Is there any permanent damage?"

"Well that is hard to say right now. The swelling in her brain has gone down dramatically but it is still swollen so it is hard to say."

"Is she going to wake up soon," Mama asked trying not to break down. Dad went over to be with her.

"All we can do is wait. I must tell you that the longer she is unconscious indicates a moderate to severe amount of injury."

"Will she be able to walk and talk normally," my dad asked.

"Again, all we can do is wait. However, it is very likely that she will have post-traumatic amnesia and her ability to talk and move depends on how much damage there is to the brain."

"Who could do this?" my mom asked hysterically.

"I'm sorry this has happened to your daughter Mrs. Robinson," Detective Myers said. "We have a few leads but nothing definite. I'll call you soon as I find anything."

My mom went home to be with the kids and rest and I stayed at the hospital with Renee. I held back tears as I looked at my sister, wondering who could be so vicious.

"Hey girl," Kina said as she walked in with a bouquet of flowers, "Alexis told me what happened; how are you holding up?"

"Okay I guess," I said sitting them on the window sill with the others. "With everything that's been going on, I haven't seen you in a while."

"I know."

"What are you all dressed up for, surely not the hospital," I joked.

"I was headed to a party at my neighbor's house, but I rushed over here as soon as I heard about Renee."

"There's not much we can do right now but wait. Don't let me ruin your evening, I'm fine…really."

"You aren't ruining anything. Besides we need to catch up. I can still go later."

"So, are you taking a date?" I asked wanting to take my mind off what was going on here.

"Just Alexis, but she had to take care of something with her family."

"I'm glad you came."

"Me too," she replied taking a seat next to me.

Chapter 7

Alexis

I cannot believe I let Trina talk me into sneaking into Eugene's house. My heart was racing as we turned onto his street.
"Park around the block," Trina suggested.
"I'm not sure about this," I said as I parked the car on the next street over and turned off the engine. "Maybe Kina is right, we should just wait and see if he even finds the letter or brings it up."
"Would you relax, it's not like you're stealing anything. Besides you might get some insight like the MTV show Room Raiders."
"Whatever, let's just get in and get out. I'm not trying to be here that long."
We put our hoodies up on our head as we walked back to Eugene's place. We knocked on the door before we tried anything. I fumbled with the credit card until Trina took over. She jimmied the lock in one swipe.
"I take this isn't your first break-in."
"If I told you, I'd have to kill you," she said jokingly and entered the house.
"This place is nice, you sure he's straight?" she asked.

"Positive," I said closing and locking the door behind me. "C'mon, I think he put my purse in here," I said heading towards one of the bedrooms.

Trina sat down on the bed.

"I could live here," she said making herself comfortable.

"Would you get off the bed, we aren't here to relax. C'mon help me look for the envelope."

We searched the room, scanned the floor, under the bed, and checked the closet.

"Maybe it was another room," Trina said as she went to the master bedroom.

I followed her inside and scanned the room. My heart sank as I saw an open envelope on the dresser.

"Is that it?" she asked as I picked it up and started to read its contents:

Alexis,

I don't want to stop seeing each other. I know we have only been dating a couple of months now, but I can tell that you are someone special. I want to see where this relationship goes, long distance or not. Give me a call once you get this.

Isaiah

"Oh my God, he read this. I hope he doesn't think I'm playing him."

"Let me see it," Trina said snatching the note and skimming it over. "Just tell him the truth, y'all broke up and now he's trying to get you back."

"Well, we never officially broke up."

"He don't know that, besides," Trina was interrupted by the sound of keys turning the lock of the front door. She threw her finger up to her mouth to quiet me as if I could utter a sound.

"We gotta hide," I whispered looking for somewhere feasible. We both ran into the closet. I was certain he heard the commotion of us knocking hangers around.

"You need any help with your bags," I heard Eugene ask.

"Nah, man I got it," Lance replied.

I shut the closet door as quietly as possible but left it cracked so I could keep a look-out.

"Hey G, you got an extra t-shirt."

"Yeah, let me go grab it."

"Oh snap," I uttered before I knew it.

Trina shushed me again and I closed the door a little more. I heard his foot steps getting closer to where we were and I prayed that the shirt he was going for wasn't in the closet. I opened the door about half an inch and saw him going through the dresser. He grabbed a shirt from the drawer and paused to look at the dresser. He looked around and I knew he had to be searching for the note. My heart pounded and I was certain he could hear it. Thankfully he left the room.

"Here you go bruh. What time you need to go to the airport."

"Not until later on tonight."

"Dag," Trina mumbled behind me.

"I'm hungry, what you got to eat."

"It's some hot dogs in there."

"It's pretty out; let's throw them on the grill. It could be my going away dinner."

"You already had a going away dinner. But we could do that."

"Yo, you should call that chick back over here again, and see if she got a friend?"

"Who Alexis?"

"Nah, the shorty that was over here before that."

"Aight."

I heard his footsteps approach the room again. I watched as he searched his room for something, probably the note. Just as I thought he was coming to the closet, his phone rang.

"I was literally just about to call you," I heard him say to the caller. He talked with her for about a few minutes and I felt stupid about worrying about my note and he was seeing somebody else.

"Yo Lance, that was old girl just now. She's on her way."

"She bringing anybody with her?"

"Yeah she said she's with her cousin."

"Cool, we better go set up the grill."

I heard the door open and close yet I still paused.

"It's now or never," Trina said pushing me out the closet.

"What if they see us," I asked. We heard the door open back up and rushed the closet again.

"Grab some ground beef too," Lance called out.

"Let me change first."

"Crap," Trina mumbled.

"You oughta change after you cook so you won't mess your clothes up," Lance suggested.

"True."

We both breathed a sigh of relief. I heard fumbling in the kitchen then the door opened and closed again. We exited the closet and peeked out the bedroom door. Soon we heard laughing outside and Trina motioned for me to follow her.

"Wait," I said.

"We don't have time."

"I need to put the note back. I saw he was looking for it."

"So..."

"Just wait a minute."

I slid the note partially under the dresser so he would think it fell. Then we tiptoed out the room and made our way to the living room. I heard Lance come in again and we froze. Before I could react, Trina was out the front door and I hurried behind her shutting it as quickly and quietly as possible. Then I high tailed after her.

"You think they saw us," she asked as we got back to the car.

"I don't know," I answered just above a whisper.

I hadn't heard from Eugene since our dinner date and I refused to call after everything I heard. Even though I said I didn't want a relationship, I was still upset that he was talking to someone else. I busied myself at work trying not to think about the situation.

"I'm sorry about the other day," Missy said at the end of our shift. "I was in a funky mood with the break-up and my kids' father acting crazy. I didn't mean to take it out on you."

"Don't sweat it. I'm sorry I blew up."

"Let's go out to dinner then. Do you want to go to that Mexican restaurant again?"

"No, let's try someplace else," I responded remembering our last time there. "How about Outback?"

"That sounds good; just let me change first."

After our last outing I was worried to see her outfit. I breathed a sigh of relief when she came out wearing some designer jeans and a t-shirt.

"Hold on a minute," Jerry stopped us as we were headed out. "Didn't those jeans just come in today?" he asked looking at Missy.

"Yeah," she answered.

"Well, what are you doing with them on? I didn't see you buy anything today."

"Well I did. I don't know why you're sweating me about it. If it will make you feel any better, here," she said throwing a couple of bills that wouldn't cover the jeans alone.

"I'll meet you later," I said sensing the drama about to ensue.

"No, just wait a minute," Jerry responded, "did you know about this?"

"No."

"This isn't the first time she's done this. Are you saying you never saw her take anything?"

"That's exactly what I'm saying," I responded not hiding my aggravation at what he was implying.

"Well, Missy, you're fired… and Alexis I'm suspending you until Bridgette can do an investigation. I'm sure she would be interested in knowing what her new 'manager' is involved in."

"What! I'm not involved in anything. Besides, if you knew she was stealing why didn't you say anything before? I hope this doesn't have anything to do with me not going out with you."

"Please, you are feeling yourself too much. And just so you know, I'll be calling Bridgette first thing Monday so you may as well forget about going in for training."

"Oh, this is some bull," Missy interjected, "She didn't have anything to do with this and you know it."

"I don't know anything; besides, that's for Bridgette to find out after she has the tapes reviewed."

Detective Myers

The tapes from the hotel didn't exactly incriminate Kenneth with anything but it did make him our number one suspect. We brought him back in for questioning and hoped to get enough on him to charge him and get another dead beat off the street.

"You lied to me Kenneth. Not only do you know Renee but you were having an affair with her."

"Okay, I know her but I didn't do anything to her."

"Then why did you lie?" I said slapping the table with a little too much aggression but I held my ground.

"Because I knew she was missing and my past charges didn't look good for me. Besides, you had your mind made up that I was guilty before you brought me in here."

"When was the last time you saw Renee?"

"I don't know... Maybe a couple of weeks ago."

"How about March 2nd, at the Holiday Inn. The day she went missing."

"Look, I picked her up from work and we went to my hotel room but she left and I don't know what happened after that."

"I think you do know. Renee told you it was over and you went after her," I said as I slammed the evidence photos on the table.

"Oh no! I didn't do this. I would never…" he replied showing emotion over the photos. It still wasn't enough to convince me he didn't do it.

"Actually, you have. It's your same MO. The girl gets ready to leave and you don't like that so you make sure she doesn't."

"It's not like that. She thought I was cheating on her so she left. I swear I didn't touch her."

"Why would she think that?"

"Well my ex must have followed us and she knocked on the room door. Before I could explain to Renee that we weren't together anymore she left."

"When you say ex, are you talking about Tammy?"

"No."

"Well I need a name."

I got the information from him and then Eric walked in with some information from the search we did on his vehicle.

"It looks like you are lying again Kenneth. The lab Techs found blood trace in your car. So what really happened, did you go after her?"

"You got it twisted; I told you I didn't have anything to do with Renee."

"So how did blood end up in your car?"

"I got into a fight with someone from… I'm not saying anything until my lawyer Brian Crawley gets here."

Kina

Just as I was about to leave the dinner party at my neighbor's house, the Dillard's, I saw Tyler walking in.
"What are you doing here?" I asked, trying not to speak too loudly. I glanced across the parking lot to see if Alexis was back yet. I let out a sigh of relief when I didn't see her car.
"The lady next door to you said you were across the street and I assumed she meant this party?"
"Why are you looking for me? I told you that I want to move past what happened."
"I know, can we talk outside?" he asked his eyes pleading.
Reluctantly I followed him outside.
"What is it?" I asked.
"I know you said that you want to move on but I can't. When we were together I just opened up to you. I've never been so honest with anyone in my life and…"
"You can stop right there. I don't care about that; you need to let this go I can't…"
"Kina," he interrupted, "tell me you didn't feel a connection between us."
"I did, but this is wrong. I can't do this to Sherri, especially now with her sister hanging on by a thread."

"So they found her?" he asked shocked. "I wonder why she didn't tell me."

"Maybe you should be talking to her. I went by to see her and she needs a true friend right now and I want to be that for her. So chemistry or not, we have to let this go, now."

I turned and walked towards my apartment, resisting the urge to run. The apartment was a blur as I ran to the couch and plopped face down releasing my frustration out on my pillows until I fell limp and continued sobbing gently. Memories of that night haunted me, making me feel horrible for feeling a connection to him. My phone rang several times in the other room but I couldn't bring myself to move.

The sound of keys and the door opening startled me and I realized I had fallen asleep. I quickly sat up and tried to brush my hair back with my hand.

"Are you all right? I've been calling you for a minute?" Alexis stared at me with worry painted all over her face.

"I'm good?" I finally replied.

"I was worried about you. You sure you're okay, you look a mess?" she asked as she walked over and had a seat next to me on the couch.

I tried to play it cool but I knew Alexis could tell when something is up.

"I'll be okay. You still talking to Eugene," I asked shifting the focus off myself.

"Oh, let me tell you," she said turning toward me grabbing all my attention. "It turns out that I did leave the letter at his house"

"How do you know? Did he confront you about it?"

"Trina and I snuck in his house to get it back but he had already read it."

"You did what," I yelled grabbing a pillow and throwing it at her.

"The worse part is he came home while we were in there. We hid in the closet until the coast was clear and we got out before he saw us."

"I can't believe you snuck in this man's house! Have you talked to him since?"

"No, he hasn't called me and I haven't run into him at the office. Anyway, while I was there I overheard him inviting some other chick over and I felt stupid for tripping over Isaiah's note."

"Are you going to see him again?"

"I don't know. I mean we aren't officially dating but it still stings. I thought we connected at his house but I guess not."

"Listen to you, you didn't even want to get into a relationship and now look at you."

"I know. But I'm not going to trip about it. The truth is I don't need to be getting involved with anyone at work anyway so it's good I found out."

"You remember that guy I was telling you about," I brought up needing to confide in someone.

"The one with the girlfriend? Please tell me you aren't still messing with him."

"No but I keep thinking about the whole situation. He told me that he's breaking up with his girl and he wants to be with me and I feel bad because I even considered it."

"How long have you known this dude?"

"Since college…"

"Do I know him?"

"Yes…"

"Well who is it?"

"You can't tell anyone." She shook her head as if to say of course.

"It was Tyler," I blurted and dropped my face in my hands fighting back tears.

"Wait, no," she muttered in disbelief. "When did this happen; *why* did this happen?" she frantically asked.

All the excuses I used to reason with myself seemed pathetic at the moment. I guess they always were. "It just happened," I offered.

"No don't give me that. Slipping a cuss word in front of your mom just happens, dropping your plate and breaking just happens, but sleeping with your girl's man…"

"I know, don't you think I beat myself up thinking about it. It wasn't planned; I never thought it would happen until it did."

"Kina this is bad," she said. I finally looked at her and saw the hurt and disgust in her eyes. "So this is the guy you were talking about the other day, with the girlfriend," she asked knowingly.

"Yeah," I responded. She raised her eyebrows signaling that she was waiting on me to explain myself. "I ran into him at the store," I continued, "he was stressed with finals and I offered to bring him a plate. It was the night we had the spaghetti dinner at Sherri's. Anyway, I dropped off the plate and one thing led to another."

"I can't believe this. I don't know what to say," she said getting up from the chair.

"I know you are mad…"

"Disappointed is more like it," she interrupted. "I just don't understand. I know you are upset about Micah but you could have any other guy you want."

"Not everyone is as strong as you Lexie," I snapped back. "We don't all have two, three guys checking for us all the time. Look, I know I was wrong and I ended it. But, please don't judge me right now, I've already condemned myself. I just really need your support right now. I think I already lost two friends with this one; I don't want to lose you too."

She paused before responding. My eyes pleaded with her and eventually her face softened.

"This is not acceptable Kina." Her words were stern but I could still feel her heart wasn't totally closed off.

"I know," I conceded. Slowly I slid my hand closer to her on the couch. "Thicker than blood," I offered hoping I still had my friend. It was a phrase we came up with meaning that we were the closest of friends. She shook her head then finally offered her hand. "Thicker than blood," she repeated.

Alexis

Bridgette called me Monday to tell me what I already expected; that this situation won't be cleared up in time for me to start my training. She did say that she doesn't believe that I'm involved and that she's willing to relocate me until this investigation is cleared up. I was just happy to still have a job. I spent the day looking for apartments in the area and I found a nice gated neighborhood that I liked. Even with all the drama, I don't mind staying with Kina but we still need our own space. While I was looking at the apartment I got a call from Eugene.

"What's up with you, I haven't seen you since dinner."

"Not much, what about you," I asked knowingly.

"Same ol'. So what are you doing this weekend?"

"I don't know; I take it you have something in mind."

"Well, I don't know if you like sports but I have some tickets to the football game at WSSU and I would love it if you came with me."

"Sure, that sounds great. By the way, did I happen to leave a note at your house? I couldn't find it," I finally addressed the situation.

"I didn't find anything; I hope it wasn't anything important."

"Not really, I got a note from my ex' and I lost it. I'm not going to worry about it too much."

"I'm glad you lost it then. He had his shot; It's my turn to slam dunk this one."

"Is that right." I was surprised at how touched I was by the comment. Especially since I made my mind up to move on.

Missy called several times while I was on the phone but I was not ready to deal with her yet. Lex also called and left a voicemail telling me to call as soon as I got the message. I decided to drop by his house instead. On the way to his place I passed Glam to see it engulfed in flames. Shock took over and I drove even faster to his house.

"Where have you been? The police have been looking for you; I've been looking for you," Lex asked before I could get out of my car.

"I went to find an apartment…What's up?"

"Your store was on the news and they weren't sure if it was empty before the fire started…I didn't know if you were in there or not."

"Why are the police looking for me? I hope they don't think I had anything to do with this."

"They didn't say. Don't worry my lawyer, Brian Crawley, is on the way. He's going to represent you if they try to charge you with anything."

"You didn't have anything to do with this, did you?" I asked.

"Man no, how could you even ask me something like that. I'm upset that they trying to play you but I wouldn't risk your life or getting you in trouble."

"I know, I'm sorry." I replied, upset that I even questioned him. My brother is over protective but I know he's not psychotic.

Lex waited with me back at Kina's apartment for the lawyer. I called Kina to tell her what was going on but she didn't pick up her cell or work phone. Before Crawley could contact me the police were bringing me in for questioning. They took me in a little room and it took what seemed like an hour before a chubby police officer came in with a slimmer detective named Pierce. It took me a minute but I realized he was the same detective that I talked to about the anonymous notes.

"I understand you were fired recently."

"I'm not saying anything until my lawyer gets here."

"Why am I not surprised? Just like a Moretti. What other things have you picked up from the family?"

I just looked at him in silence. Upset and wondering what he was alluding to.

"I understand you don't want to talk."

They got up and walked out. Not long after they left another detective came in.

"I already told your partner that I'm not talking until my lawyer gets here."

"He's not my partner. I'm Detective Myers," she said as she extended her hand. I just looked at it. "Okay, do you know Renee Robinson?"

"Yes, I know her."

"So you know what happened to her."

"Yes and I didn't have anything to do with that either."

"Do you know what you were doing March 2nd when she disappeared?"

"I don't know; I think baby-sitting and no where near her."

"For Missy Romano?"

"Yeah, how did you know...She didn't have anything to do with it either she was on a date."

Just then Lex's lawyer came in.

"That's enough if you aren't charging her with anything then we are leaving."

"No, we got all we need, she's free to go."

He asked me what questions they had asked me and if I said anything. I told him that I didn't say anything until right before he came in and they tricked me into giving up info on Missy. Crawley gave me his card so that I could call him in case they brought me in again.

Sherri

"Hey love, how are you holding up," Tammy asked as she entered my apartment.

"I'm okay. Where are the kids?"

"They are with Kenny. I wanted to talk in private. Have they done the DNA testing on Renee and Derrick yet?"

"Yeah, how did you know?"

"Because they think Kenny is the father. They questioned me. Since he had an affair with her they thought I might have attacked Renee for revenge."

"Oh my gosh, that is ridiculous. I cannot believe he could be the father. All this time and neither of them said anything."

"Guilt probably. I don't care about that so much as having to explain it to the kids. How is Renee?"

"About the same. She woke up once, though. Mom was there. I had to work. I'm going back over there in a minute."

"Have you heard from Kina or Tyler?"

"Kina visited me at the hospital. I haven't talked to Tyler yet. I'm surprised he hasn't called me. Why do you ask?"

"Just curious. Well I have to go pick up the kids. Call me and let me know how Renee is doing."

I headed to the hospital as soon as Tammy left. My mom was asleep in the chair next to Renee; she jumped as I walked in. "How's she doing?" I asked. I could tell my mom hadn't been resting. With everything that has happened I'm concerned of her health.
"She's been waking up off and on. She tries to talk but when she does it's not understandable. Dr. Water's came in and they did some more tests."
"So what did they find out? Is she going to be able to walk, and talk normally?"
"She said it's still too soon to know for sure and that it's normal for her to be awake for only moments at a time at first."

Renee woke up once while I was there but she didn't say much. The doctors said not too push her and to let her rest. Mom stayed at the hospital and Dad watched the kids. I went home to have a moment to myself. Teresa, Kina's neighbor and wannabe friend, called me claiming she wanted to see how everyone was doing but more than likely wanted to pry into our business.
"I'm glad to hear that your sister is showing signs of progress. When Tammy told me what was going on I had to call. Please let me know if you need anything… a meal, a baby-sitter anything."
"Thanks so much, Teresa. Right now I'm just trying to get some rest."

"I understand. I know this is a tough time for you, especially having to deal with a break-up while your sister is in the hospital."

"Break-up?"

"Oh…you and Tyler are still together?"

"He hasn't said anything to me."

"Well, I hate I brought it up."

"Please tell me if you know something." Teresa isn't exactly a reliable source but I still wanted to hear what she had to say.

"I just assumed you weren't together anymore when I saw him out with someone else at the Dillard's party this past Sunday. I'm sure it's nothing."

"Well, who was he with?" I asked frantically, Tyler never mentioned anything about going to a party let alone that he was taking someone. When she told me who he was with, I almost lost consciousness myself.

Tammy

I hadn't heard from Stephanie since the weekend so I walked over to her building during lunch.

"How you doing?" I asked.

"Good. I've been meaning to call you—I just been so busy lately."

"Did everything work out with Jonathan?"

"He's called a couple times but he still hasn't seen J.B. again; Brad doesn't think it's a good idea."

"Well it's not about what Brad thinks. Did you at least tell J.B. his father wants to know him?"

"Look, don't come over here judging me. I'm not going to let Jonathan mess up a good relationship because of his mistakes."

"I'm not judging you and I could care less about Jonathan or Brad; I care about J.B. I know what it is like growing up without a father and I would hate for him to go through that if he doesn't have to."

"I'm doing what's best for both of us; Brad has been great to J.B."

"But he's not his father; I had a stepfather growing up too and I loved him but it still hurt that my biological father never wanted to see us. If he was really great then he would understand that."

"Why you want to get me in trouble with Brad, huh. You know he was right; you are just jealous because your marriage didn't work."

"Are you kidding me? I'm not jealous of your relationship; I know what it is like to make sacrifices for love and I can tell you one thing, love isn't supposed to hurt. Look at you; you are cheating your son out of knowing his father and talking about getting in trouble. You are not his child."

"Please, just drop it. I know Brad loves us and in time he will warm up to J.B. meeting his father once he sees that he can trust me."

"If he truly loves you he should already trust you. I just don't want to see you get hurt."

"I know what I'm doing okay. Everything is going to be fine."

Chapter 8

Alexis

After the interrogation I called Lex to tell him how it went. He was just glad my name was free and clear of the fire at the store. He told me he was working, but I went to see Trina and the baby anyway.

"Can you watch Alexia until Missy gets here? I booked the studio for 11 and you know Lex doesn't like to lose time and money."

"Sure. What time is she supposed to get here? I have a date later on tonight."

"She was supposed to be here at ten; it's almost eleven now. But, I should be back by three."

"No problem; I don't mind looking after my niece," I replied and took the baby from her.

"So, who are you seeing tonight?" Trina asked with a slick smile on her face.

"Eugene, he called and asked me to a game at WSSU."

"You going out with him even though you know he's talking to someone else?"

"Well, we aren't officially together," I defended.

"So why in the world did you have us playing I-Spy at his house over a note?"

"I don't know; it's complicated."

"You know Ka$h still asks about you."

"And..."

"He's a cool dude I don't know why you flexing on him."

"I'm not trying to get caught up with an artist. Besides he doesn't even know me; I'm sure the only thing he wants is some booty."

"I don't know about that but it's your call. Anyway, I appreciate you doing this for me. Tell Missy to call me whenever she gets here."

Missy arrived at noon and she seemed distracted.

"Hey girl! Sorry I'm late; hope you weren't here long."

"Nah, I just..."

"Cool," she interrupted. "How's everything going with you? You working at the new store yet?"

"Not until next week. Are you feeling okay? I don't mind watching her," I probed sensing the tension.

"I wasn't feeling too good this morning, but I'm cool. You go have fun."

I texted Trina and let her know that Missy finally came and I headed over to the hospital to see how Renee was doing before my date with Eugene. When I got there no one was in the room and

Renee was asleep. She had all kinds of flowers and balloons decorating the pale hospital room. I was just about to leave when Sherri came in with a cup of coffee.

"I'm glad you came. I was getting a little restless."

Sherri wore bags around her eyes and a wrinkled pantsuit.

"Did you spend the night here?" I asked noticing the blankets over in the corner window.

"Yeah. Renee has been staying awake for longer periods of time now. I wanted to be here in case she woke up again."

"Oh that's great. Is she talking yet?"

"A little. She doesn't remember anything about the attack and she needs help to remember things but at least we can understand her now."

"I remember the doctor saying that she would probably have amnesia. Any luck finding out who did this?" I asked.

"Not yet. Detective Myers says they think they know who done this but they are still looking for her."

"It's a woman?"

"Yeah, they think that she was jealous of Renee because she was seeing her old boyfriend."

"Oh. It's a shame that it went this far."

While I was sitting with Renee, Detective Myers came in.

"Any new developments?" Sherri asked.

"Not yet, we are still looking for her?"

"Excuse my manners, Detective; this is my friend Alexis" Sherri introduced.

"We've met," I answered callously remembering our last encounter.

"I'm glad you're here, Alexis. Do you know where Missy is?"

"You know the woman that did this?" Sherri asked upset.

"Missy is my cousin, but she didn't do this."

"Missy isn't who you think she is. Did you know she is a Bipolar Schizophrenic?" Myers asked.

"No..." The information was a shock but I still wasn't going to allow her to muscle anymore information out of me.

"She was arrested for assault before in DC and she has been off her meds since she's been in Winston. If you know how to contact her please let us know. She's needs help."

"Look I aint no snitch; besides how do you know that she's done this... because Kenny said so, please. She was on a date that night with her ex KD."

"Alexis if you know something please tell her," Sherri pleaded with me.

"KD, huh. Kenneth Dwayne James..." Detective Myers probed. Once I figured out that K.D. was Tammy's ex I almost fell to the floor. I realized that when Missy said K.D. was upset because she flipped on him she was probably talking about when she attacked Renee. I know I shouldn't snitch, especially on family, but at the same time I owe it to Renee to tell her where she is. I gave Detective Myers Missy's address and number and after she left I remembered that she was baby-sitting Lexie. I called Trina to see if she left the studio yet.

"Hey Trina; you been to the house to get Lexie yet?"

"What you mean? Missy called and said she left her with you?"

"No, I left them both at the house?"

"I'm at the house and they aren't here… She probably just took her out for a walk or something she's been fussy lately."

"I hope that's all it is."

"Why, is something wrong?"

"I don't know yet. I'll call you later."

I left the hospital to go see if I could find Missy and Lexie. Crazy or not, if she did anything to my niece the police will be the last thing Missy has to worry about.

Tammy

When Sherri told me that they found out who attacked Renee, I was glad to hear that it wasn't Kenny. The kids were just warming up to him and I don't know how they would have reacted to their father being in prison again. I figured I should tell them about Derrick being their brother, but I can never get up the nerve. Kenny took Rod to get a haircut earlier today. I met them outside when they got back.

"Go inside with your sister so I can talk with your Dad."

"What's up?" Kenny asked.

"When are you going to tell the kids about Derrick?"

"About that…Tammy, I'm sorry."

"Don't apologize to me. We were over a long time ago; you don't owe me anything… So, when are you going to tell them?"

"I don't know. Maybe you should tell them."

"Why me; this is your mess."

"I know but Janise already don't trust me."

"That's why you need to be honest with her. Trust me it will be better if it came from you."

"I guess so... Do you forgive me?"

"I'll have the kids call you later. Maybe you can pick them up from school next week and explain it to them."

I was finishing up dinner when I heard a knock on the door. I answered it and saw Sherri looking tired as usual lately and a little upset.

"How are you doing?" she asked.

"I'm doing. I'm finishing up dinner now, you want to stay and eat with us?"

"I'm not that hungry."

"Yeah but you still have to eat. I bet you haven't eaten at all today."

"Not in the last couple of days. I've been so stressed out."

"I thought Renee was getting better."

"She is, but it's still too early to know how much she's going to recover plus the drama with Tyler is eating away at me, I guess we are finally breaking up."

"Really?"

"I haven't heard it from him but if what I know about him and Kina is true; it's a wrap."

"So she finally told you?" I asked.

"Yeah, Teresa called to comfort me over the break-up that I didn't know about. Wait a minute, she told you first? See I don't even know if I can believe Teresa, she's always instigating something…"

"No," I interjected, "I haven't talked to Teresa; I mean I figured Kina told you."

"I haven't talked to either of them. But why do you say finally like you knew all along?"

"I didn't mean it like that," I lied. I couldn't admit I knew and didn't say anything. "Did the police ever find the girl that they think is responsible?" I asked hoping she would drop it. I wasn't trying to get caught in the middle.

"I don't know. Can you believe that it is Alexis' cousin? She came by the hospital today and gave Myers the address she had on her but I haven't heard from either of them since."

"Did Alexis know all this time?"

"I don't think so. Have you talked to Janise and Rod about Derrick?"

"No, I'm going to let Kenny tell them. What about the girls, do they know?"

"Not yet. We finally let them come to the hospital to see their mom since she's been waking up. It broke my heart watching the pain in their eyes when they saw her like that."

"Girl, you know I'm here for you and if you are going to stand strong than you need to eat."

I called the kids down so we could all eat together. I had Janise help me set the table and I convinced Sherri to eat something too.

"Janise put that phone up," I said almost ready to take it away. Ever since Kenny bought that thing she has had her face into it.

"I didn't know you had a phone," Sherri attempted to be upbeat.

"Yeah, I called you to give you my number but I couldn't reach you."

"I'm sorry. I've been busy lately," Sherry replied.

"I understand; it's cool," Janise assured her.

"I got a phone too," Rod added enthusiastically.

"Oh that's nice."

"Yeah, his dad got him a TracFone. Janise, I told you to put that phone up. Don't make me take it."

"Sorry. Somebody keeps calling me from a private number and hanging up."

"Well, who have you given your number to?" I asked.

"Nobody really."

"Just don't answer it," Sherri suggested.

We finished dinner and the phone vibrated the whole time. Sherri barely touched her food. She stayed for a little while then went back to the hospital to be with her family. I straightened up the house a little bit and went upstairs to tell the kids to clean their rooms. When I got upstairs Janise's phone was ringing again.

"Let me answer it…Hello!"

"You think you slick not answering the phone. You better stay away from my man, we got a baby now." The caller demanded.

"Excuse me! You got the wrong number," I said then hung up.

She called right back, "don't be hanging up on me. This is the right number because I found it in K.D,'s phone. You better not call him anymore."

"You must me crazy. Don't be calling here threatening nobody; this is his daughter's phone."

This time she hung up. I called Kenny to tell him a thing or two about his new line of women, but he didn't answer.

Just when I thought things would finally calm down, Stephanie was at my door. I could tell she had been crying.

"What's the matter?" I asked after I let her in.

"He took him; he just took him and I can't do anything about it."

"What are you talking about?"

"Well I haven't been answering Jonathan's calls so he found him a lawyer. He called and demanded that I tell J.B. about who he really was. I talked to my mom about letting him visit J.B. at her house and she agreed. So I took J.B. over there and Brad found out about it and met us over there. He started yelling at me and Jonathan and saying that he was J.B.'s father and that Jonathan would never see him if he had anything to do with it. Jonathan took J.B. with him and the police said that I never got sole custody and there is nothing I could do until we go to court."

"Oh no," I said hugging her and I could feel her flinch in my arms. "What's wrong?"

"I hurt my arm; it's still sore."

"Did he put his hands on you?"

"Me and Brad are fine; I just need to get my son back."

"You are not fine; you need to let him go so that you can get your son back with you."

"Brad loves me; it happened in the commotion of everything. It was a mistake.."

"That's what they all say; if he did it once he will do it again. Steph it's only going to get worse."

"You don't know anything. Just because your husband abused you doesn't mean every man is out to hurt women. Look, I came over here for a friend not a critic; I just want my son back."

Sherri

After I left Tammy's house I went home to get some rest before I had to go get the kids from my mom. Detective Myers called to tell me that they went to search Missy's place. They found DNA evidence linking her to the attack and they also found gasoline in her garbage receptacle which makes them think she had something to do with the fire at Glam. I just hope that they catch up with her before she does anything to someone else. I called Alexis to make sure she was okay, but I couldn't get her. Not long after I got settled in I got a call from Tyler.

"I'm sorry it took me so long to call you back; I've been really busy."

"I bet," I replied. The sound of his voice irritated me. I didn't realize how angry I was until he called.

"You sound a upset; is your sister doing any better?"

"She's progressing. How was the Dillard's party?"

"It was okay"

"Who did you go with?"

"Nobody… is something wrong?"

"I don't know you tell me."

"I don't know what you're talking about."

"I'm talking about you and Kina at the party; imagine my surprise when Teresa called to comfort me over our break-up. How could you?"

"It's not what you think."

"I think you are sneaking around with my best friend."

"Look it's nothing serious; I was going to tell you the other day but there was so much going on with your sister and then she was at the hospital—It wasn't a good time to tell you."

"It's never a good time to tell someone that you are seeing their best friend."

"We never planned this to happen. You are always so busy with the kids and your sister and you aren't there for me. And now it looks like you may have them full time; I'm not ready for that burden."

"And that makes it okay!" I shouted. "You shouldn't treat anyone like that, especially someone who has been a friend to you since," my emotions overwhelmed me.

"Just listen…"

"Whatever, I don't even want to talk about it anymore."

I was upset with Tyler but even more so with Kina. We have been friends for five years and now she wants to throw that away for this. I called her as soon as I hung up.

"Hey girl," she answered.

"How could you?"

"What?"

"You know what I'm talking about?"

"I'm sorry; we were going to tell you but…"

"But nothing! We were supposed to be friends. You listened to me pour my heart out to you and you didn't say anything. You are trifling."

"Sherri wait… I told Tammy I was going to tell you, I was just waiting for the right time."

"Save it—y'all deserve each other."

I hung the phone up even more angry that Tammy was being so secretive at the house and she already knew what was going on. I threw my phone across the room and it shattered. I thought about confronting Tammy to ask her why she didn't say anything but my I didn't have the strength. I realized everyone must have known about Tyler and Kina but me. They were all smiling in my face like nothing is wrong. And they call themselves my 'sisters'.

Alexis

I called Missy's phone as soon as I left the hospital but she didn't pick up. I rushed to her house to see if she was there. Detective Myers stopped me in the yard.

"You can't go in while they are searching the place."

"Is she in there?"

"No, but her kids were here by themselves."

"Oh no. Was there a newborn in there?"

"No, just Miyah and Miguel. Did she have a baby recently?"

"No," I retorted. I turned to leave and grabbed my phone to call Lex and Trina.

"Alexis," she called after me. I kept moving hoping she wouldn't follow. Once in my car I dialed Lex's number. The detective slowly headed back towards the house so I finally pulled away towards Lex's house.

Trina answered and I let her know everything I heard from the detective.

"Oh my God; and she's got my baby!"

"I think I have an idea where she might be. I'll be there to get you in a minute."

When I got to Lex and Trina's they were outside waiting on me. Trina had on a jogging suit and a scarf on her head.

"C'mon we gone ride in the Expedition," Lex insisted.

"You don't even know where we're going," I contested.

"I will when you tell me."

I saw there was no point arguing and hopped in the jeep. "I think she might be at Kenny's house in Greensboro."

"K.D.," he asked. "I know exactly where that's at."

Lex sped off and I pried for more information. "The police said that Missy is crazy or something and off her meds. I mean you grew up with her, did you know she was off?"

"Missy is a little eccentric but she ain't crazy. I never known her to need any medicine. That's probably some mess the police cooked up."

"I hope that's all it is," I replied for Trina's benefit but I wasn't so sure.

"I don't know but if everything's not on the up and up when I get there with my baby, I'm rocking that head," Trina added, her foot rapidly tapping.

"Let's just calm down and see what's up when we get there," Lex replied.

"How do you know Kenny," I asked.

"Barely, he has done some work down at the studio. I knew he hooked up with Missy but he said that was over. Wait, how you know this dude," he asked looking at me in his mirror.

"He's married to my friend Tammy, for now anyway."

"Hmm," was all he offered.

We made the twenty minute trip in what seemed like five. As we pulled up and saw Missy's car out front. Trina was about to hop out and run in but Lex stopped her.

"Y'all wait in the car."

"My baby is in there; I'm not staying out here," Trina said already out the car.

Once we were outside we could here Missy and Kenny arguing.

"Girl you must be crazy, I told you it is over. Now you need to leave."

"But we have a baby; you can't do me like this."

"I don't know where you got that baby from but you need to get out of here before I call the police."

"But I love you," Missy pleaded and was interrupted by Trina banging on the door, Lex posted up behind her. Everything got quiet and then Kenny called out, "Who is it?"

"It's me Trina, open up!"

"You better not open it," Missy yelled.

"What you mean," Trina yelled through the door. It got quiet again and so Trina ran to the side of the house to see if she could see anything through the windows. We could barely see anything so I ran to the other side to get a better look. I could see Missy with Lexie in her arms and a blade up to her insisting that Kenny go upstairs.

"Oh snap," I waved Trina and Lex over to see what was happening.

"You better not touch my baby," Trina yelled and Lex ran to kick in the door. As soon as he kicked it in Detective Myers rolled up with her troop and Trina rushed in the house.

"Did you call the police," Lex asked upset.

"No," I answered.

"Step away from the house," I heard a large man with graying hair. I assumed it was the police captain.

Reluctantly we obliged; then we heard screaming from upstairs. Lex ran to see what was going on but deputy all American stopped him and insisted we wait.

Detective Myers approached us, "please calm down. Is Missy in there?"

"Yes, and she has my niece," I answered.

"Who else is in there?" she asked. Kenny came out with Lexie.

"My baby," Lex yelled and ran to meet Kenny; some cops tried to stop him but weren't quick enough. Kenny handed the baby over to Lex and he just held her in his arms then checked to see if she was hurt. The detective wouldn't let me go over to them.

"Captain Discher is going to get a statement from them; tell me is Missy alone?"

"No, my sister-in-law is in there," I answered frustrated and then we heard a crash in the house. I attempted to run to see what was going on but one of the police officers grabbed me. Myers and several other cops ran in. I went over to where Lex and Kenny where.

"Man what happened?" Lex asked Kenny.

"I was on the phone with Tammy cussing me out about one of my girls calling and threatening Janise; next thing I know this crazy chick is banging on my door talking about I told you I was pregnant; not long after that y'all was at my door."

"How did you get the baby out," I asked.

"When Trina rushed in, it threw Missy off guard so I grabbed the baby and when I saw Trina was taking care of business I came out here."

Lex got on his phone to call Crawley again. The police finally came outside with Trina in handcuffs but I didn't see Myers or Missy.

"Baby don't say nothing; I'm on the phone with Crawley now," Lex yelled to Trina as they took her away.

Chapter 10

Tammy

Work was piling on my desk because I was more focused on Sherri and her sister. I tried calling her but I haven't heard back from her yet. I know she has a lot on her plate right now so I decided I would stop back after work. Once I finally got serious about my backed up work, Stephanie sent me and IM.

Steph123:How are you?

T.J.0106:Hangin in there. How's J.B.?

Steph123:O.K. He actually likes the idea of being with his father. It's killing me, though.

T.J.0106:And Brad?

Steph123:He blames me; I blame myself.

T.J.0106:Don't be so hard on yourself. When is the custody hearing?

Steph123:This afternoon.

T.J.0106You need me to go with you?

Steph123:No. Brad will be there.

T.J.0106Ok; let me know how it goes...

Stephanie's situation worries me. Brad is sending the same signs I ignored from Kenny but I don't want to keep preaching to her. I know she won't see the light until she is ready, or forced to. After work I tried Sherri again without any luck. I couldn't get Kina or Alexis on the phone either. I tried not to worry too much; I assumed that if something serious happens someone would call. Back at home I prepared dinner for the kids. Janise and Rod were in the family room watching T.V. so I took the opportunity to make myself a cocktail. With all the stress from my own drama and my girls I deserve one every day if I could. Since I couldn't get in touch with any of my girls, I decided to call Stephanie to see how the trial went.

"Hello," Brad answered her cell phone.

"May I speak with Stephanie?"

"Who is this?" he questioned.

"Tammy."

"Oh," he responded sounding mildly irritated. "She's not here."

"Okay, will you let her know I called?"

"Yeah, whatever," he said and abruptly hung up.

Stephanie is hardly without her phone so I didn't know how else to reach her. The situation seemed suspicious so I called her mom to see if she heard from her since court. Her mom said that she talked with her briefly and was supposed to stop by her house but needed to drop Brad home first. I'm surprised she left her phone behind but I would at least give her time to check in her mom before I started overreacting.

Alexis

After everything that happened with the store and my family I almost canceled my date with Eugene. But once I got home I couldn't take sitting there with Kina. She's my girl and I love her, but things have been awkward since she told me about what happened with Tyler. I shuffled through my clothes and tried on several outfits not satisfied with any of them.
"That's the one," Kina said popping her head through the door of her spare room that I have been staying in.
"You like this one," I asked looking at it again in the mirror.
"Glossy," she replied waving her hand and snapping her finger. We both gave a light chuckle.
"I'm so nervous; I don't know why," I admitted to her.
"Yeah, especially since you guys are just friends," she replied mockingly.
"Right," I retorted.
She brushed her hair from her face and for the first time since I had been home I noticed how disheveled she looked. Her eyes were baggy from crying and I felt sorry for her.
"You sure you will be ok by yourself?" I asked.
"Yeah, I'll be fine," she assured me. "Behave yourself tonight," she teased then headed down the hallway.

Eugene and I decided to ride together so I met him at his house. "Have I mentioned that you look good tonight," Eugene said on the way to the college.

"Yeah, you might have mentioned it a couple of times. But I don't mind hearing it again."

"You look lovely, by the way," he joked. "So what's been going on with you; I haven't heard from you in a while. If I didn't know any better, I would think you were dodging a brother."

"Never that," I responded. I wondered how much of my personal life I should reveal. "I've been busy with my family and work.

"So how is your mom?"

"Better. She's been busy visiting with her new grandbaby, my niece," I paused as his phone rang.

"I'm putting it on silent, continue," he said then offered a smile that made me forgive the interruption.

"That's it, really. How about you?"

"I'm boring; I spend most my time at work or researching for work."

"So is that what this is, an excuse for me to get more work done. I didn't bring my notepad," I teased.

"Not at all. I admit that I may use some info from this evening but I would use any excuse to spend more time with you."

With our press pass we had some of the best seats I've ever had at one of these games. We really had a great time together but I couldn't get past the fact that his phone kept ringing. I didn't bring it up because he never let it break the attention he gave me. Eugene went to get us some snacks and made the mistake of leaving his jacket behind. His phone rang again and I glanced behind me to make sure he wasn't coming. I slid his phone out of the pocket to see if a female name would be on the caller ID. The number came up without a name but it looked familiar for some reason. I didn't want to answer or do anything that would give away that I even looked at his phone, so I jotted the number down and put it in my purse to look at later. I put the phone back in the pocket and glanced back up to see if he was headed back. Even though I didn't see him my heart still raced with nervous excitement. Immediately I felt bad for spying, again. Being with Eugene is so comfortable yet for some reason something keeps holding me back. Maybe it's just the reporter in me. Despite my guilt from snooping we had a wonderful date.

"So when can I see you again," he asked as we sat in the car back in his driveway.

"As soon as I'm free," I honestly replied.

"I will hold you to that."

For a moment we sat taking in each other's energy and I got nervous. It has been a while since someone made me feel like I could love and it scared me.

"So call me," I stated. I felt his eyes on me as I made my way to my car but I refused to look back.

On my way back to the apartment I decided to swing by the hospital. Even though I didn't personally hurt Sherri, I felt guilty by association with Missy and Kina. The police charged Missy with assault with a deadly weapon, kidnapping, arson, and other things and is in police custody at the hospital. Trina was also charged with assault but Crawley is confident that he can get her off with the defense that she wasn't in a stable frame of mind since her newborn was kidnapped and her hormones were still out of whack.

"It's okay; how could you know," Sherri replied after I apologized for her sister's situation but I could sense some tension.

"Sherri, are you sure you're okay? You look like you haven't slept in days."

"I haven't. Things have been too stressful. The good thing is Renee is waking up more. She just went back to sleep before you came."

"I hate I missed it."

"Hey Sherri," Kina said peeping her head in the door, "can we talk?"

I almost fell out of my chair when I saw Kina enter; all I could think was it was too soon but I couldn't frame my mouth to utter any words.

"I cannot believe you had the nerve to come down here," Sherri yelled.

"Let's not do this here," I insisted unnoticed. Sherri was intently focused on Kina.

"You need to leave," Sherri asserted.

"Look, I'm really sorry, can we please talk."

"Is everything all right," one of the nurses asked walking into the room. Sherri left the room in tears and Kina followed her. I quickly grabbed my phone and headed after them while dialing Tammy's number.

"Girl we are about to get banned from the hospital," I alerted her.

"Oh lord; I knew something might go down. I told Kina it wasn't a good idea to meet her at the hospital. Just keep them calm, I'm almost there."

I walked to the end of the hall and I didn't see them so I took the elevator down to the lobby. I called both their cell phones and no luck. Finally, I found them outside in the parking lot.

"I told you I don't have anything else to say to you," Sherri yelled, "I am going through too much right now I don't have time to deal with you."

"Look, we have been friends too long to just throw it all away now. I love you like a sister," Kina pleaded and I assumed she had been drinking. I regretted leaving her at the apartment by herself.

"You came here for sympathy, please! My sister needs me right now so I cannot deal with your trifling behind."

"And you are so perfect!" Kina yelled throwing her hands up in the air.

"Kina," I interrupted, "now is not the time. Let's just go and you can talk to her later." I said taking her arm and attempting to walk away.

"Just stay out of this," she said pushing me aside. Thankfully Tammy walked up before I blanked on her.

"Kina, let's just go, we can talk about this later," Tammy pleaded with her.

"Sherri, you are so wrapped up in yourself that you never stop to see how anyone else is feeling" Kina continued.

"Excuse me; I'm sorry my problems are getting in your way," Sherri sarcastically responded and started back towards Kina.

"That's what I'm talking about. You are so selfish; you aren't the only one with problems. Every time we get together its all about you, what you have to deal with. It's no wonder Tyler couldn't talk to you about his problems."

"What," Sherri asked astounded. For a moment we were all silenced but not for long.

"That's what he wanted to talk to you about but you were so wrapped up in self-pity you couldn't hear anything else," Kina added.

"Now that's enough," Tammy interjected, "that is no excuse and it isn't going to be solved now…"

"She's right," I added. Even though I was mad at Kina's decision I shared her frustrations with Sherri's attitude. "I don't agree with what Kina did but you have been self-absorbed lately."

"Why wouldn't she be, with everything that's going on?" Tammy defended.

"Of course you would see it her way," Kina replied.

"What is that supposed to mean?"

"You always stick up for her. 'Yes Sherri, whatever you say Sherri.' You went from following orders from your husband to being stuck under Sherri's thumb," Kina argued.

"I am my own woman and I decide…"

"Yeah you decide which bottle you are going to pour down your throat for the night," Kina poked.

"Look we all have our issues; we shouldn't point fingers right now," I said trying to break the argument.

"Why because you said so or because are you worried about the blame that is coming your way," Sherri said shifting her anger at me. "After all I did to help you in college, risking my education and you are taking side with this chick!"

"Again it's all about you!" I contended. "Yes I got in some trouble during school but I never asked you for anything. Besides I have had your back plenty."

Sherri was silent but sent daggers at me with her eyes.

"Where is that coming from," Tammy asked.

"Little miss judgmental, goody two shoes should be the last one placing blame."

"I'm not perfect but at least I come from a normal family and not an episode of Soprano's," Sherri attacked."

"I can't help where I'm from and I'm not ashamed of my family. However, you should be of yourself. You keep throwing up how you were there for me but who was there for you when were too embarrassed to tell anyone you were pregnant."

"Sherri," Tammy stated inquisitively looking at Sherri for confirmation.

"Who was there for you when your lame boyfriend was so worried about his medical career that he couldn't be with you at the abortion clinic? And who was there with you when you were balling your eyes out because you kept hearing the cries of your dead baby," I continued.

"That's enough," Tammy interrupted.

"So who is really the criminal?" I asked sarcastically.

"You winch," Sherri blurted and came closer to me.

"Hypocrite," I responded returning the stare with the same intensity she was giving off.

"We should go," Kina said as she approached the two of us. I finally broke eye contact with Sherri and noticed that Kina didn't look so hot. Suddenly the alcohol she obviously partook that gave her the courage to come here made a return appearance on the pavement.

"Kina, let's get out of here," I said noticing security looking our way. "We can come back for your car later."

The car ride back to Kina's apartment was a silent one. It was soon interrupted by my cell phone ringing. I snatched it out my purse to kill the annoying ringer to see Isaiah's name. I silenced the phone and after a few seconds I thought about the number that called Eugene's phone.

"It couldn't be," I muttered.

Sherri

My sister is staying awake and talking but she has trouble remembering simple things like the day and the time. Dr. Water's said that recovery will take some time and that she will have to be in rehabilitation for a while. I'm already looking for a bigger place to accommodate the kids until Renee is self-sufficient. Her rehab specialist says that we shouldn't expect her to be the exact same as she was before the attack and that mood swings and trouble with memory is to be expected. Unfortunately I used up all my vacation time and had to return to work. I dreaded it at first, but immersing myself in work was what I needed to keep my mind off of the betrayal of my friends and the anxiety of what to do about the children. I was mad at Alexis for laying out my business, but grateful she didn't say more. As soon as I left the office I went to the hospital to check on Renee. When I arrived, she was sitting up in bed and a male nurse was checking her vitals.

"Hey Renee. How are you feeling?" I asked as I walked in and had a seat in the recliner next to the bed.

"Okay, I guess. Where's mama?"

"At home with Terra and Michele; Derrick is with Tammy."

"Who are they?" she asked. I paused, not sure of how I should respond.

"Those are your kids, Renee," I finally said with a smile, fighting to hold back my tears.

"Kids?! I don't have children?" she responded getting upset. "I'm too young to have kids."

""It's okay," the nurse said trying to calm her down. "Let's not talk about it right now," he said looking at me.

"Mama said that she will be in to see you in a little bit," I said then walked outside to catch my breath.

"It just takes time," the nurse said as he came out of the room.

"Excuse me?"

"It just takes time for her memory to come back… I'm Dylan; I'll be your sister's nurse for the evening. If you need anything just call for me."

"Thank you."

I went to go get some coffee and when I came back Renee was asleep. I sat with her until mom came in case she woke up again.

"Hey baby," my mom said as she walked in the room. "How long has she been asleep?"

"She just went."

I got up so she could sit in the chair next to Renee.

"Kina called me today," she said.

I didn't say anything hoping that would be the end of it.

"She told me about what happened," she continued. "Baby, I know they hurt you but you have to forgive them. Not for them, for you."

"Forgive them for me!" I asked using too much volume.

"Yes, for you. You keep letting this eat away at you and breaking you down. I've never seen you so low. You have too much to worry about without holding that resentment against them."

"I want to, Mama, I really do. It just hurts so badly," I cried.

She walked up and took me into her arms. I stood their crying like a child.

"I know it's hard. Have you talked to Tyler? He's called the house several times."

"Why should I," I said wiping the tears away. Before she could respond Detective Myers entered the room.

"Knock, knock," she said to signal her entrance.

"Come on in," Mama said motioning her in.

"How is Renee," she asked. She seemed genuinely concerned. I wondered if she showed this much interest in all her victims or if Renee was a special case.

"Better," I responded, "I'm fighting Tommy for temporary guardianship of the children. We go to court tomorrow."

"I wouldn't worry about it too much," Myers said reassuringly, "I doubt the judge will award him custody with the charges he is facing right now."

"Thank the Lord," Mama praised.

"I'm glad to hear that," I added.

"I wanted to let you know that we have a solid case against her attacker. I know that's not much consolation with all you are going through, but I hope it helps."

"No, it does," I responded, "thanks for all your help."

"No problem," she continued, "so have you and Alexis been friends a while?" she asked.

"Yes, why?" I asked, confused about her concern.

"Well, don't you find it odd that it was her family member that was involved? Looking at her family history…"

"Just what are you getting at?" my mom asked.

"Well the police have kept an eye on her family for quite some time and I was just wondering how you got caught up with someone like her."

"I'm going to stop you there," I said surprising myself with my defense. "Alexis has been a friend for a long time and I know she wouldn't do anything to hurt my family. No disrespect, Detective, but if you want to come in throwing allegations around, you can leave."

Tammy

I headed home to take a relaxing bath after work. Kenny picked the kids up from school and is keeping them for the weekend. He has been getting the kids every weekend, Derrick included, and keeping up with his child support. With Renee still in the hospital, I've been watching Derrick to make it easier on Sherri and her parents. She still isn't speaking with me which is tough since I have been battling my decision to continue with the divorce. That has lead me to have more 'cocktail breaks' and I thought about what Kina said at the hospital about my drinking. I have never considered myself a heavy drinker and so I wondered how it appeared to everyone else, my kids especially. So, instead of a drink I have been pampering myself in other ways. Like this bath for example. I filled the tub using my favorite bath beads but before I could get settled my phone rang.

"Tammy, have you heard from Stephanie?" Stephanie's mom, Miss Pearl asked.

"Not since yesterday. What's going on?"

"She left me a message saying that Jonathan was coming to get J.B. She sounded upset and now I can't reach her. I don't even know where Brad stays so I can't go check on her."

"I'll go by and see if she's all right" I offered and shut the water off realizing my bath was a lost cause.

"Thank you. Call me when you talk to her."

"Yes ma'am," I agreed.

I emptied the tub and headed over to his place. The lights were off but I decided to knock anyway. I barely touched the door and it came open.

"Stephanie," I called into the house. I heard someone groaning and movement inside. I grabbed my mace and entered. I called to her again as I entered further then found her lying on the floor in the hallway.

"Oh no," I gasped. I found my phone and dialed 9-1-1.

"Where is Brad?" I asked. My tears fell and mixed with the blood staining the carpet.

"It's not his fault," she muttered.

"Please, stop protecting him. You deserve better than this."

"It wasn't him," she mumbled. "J.B."

"Where is J.B.?" I asked frantically.

"Jonathan took him. He was drunk and I said he couldn't take him. So he," she couldn't finish her thought.

"Hush, the police are on the way," I said hoping to keep her calm. I was on the phone with the dispatch for a few minutes. She told me to keep Stephanie calm and I grabbed a cloth to hold pressure on the lesion on her forehead. She kept trying to talk but she was so hysterical I could hardly make out anything she was saying. Soon I heard sirens and EMS was at my side taking over. I called Miss Pearl and told her to meet us at the hospital. Two police officers came up to me while I was on the phone.

"Do you know what happened?" one of the officers asked me.

"I just got here, but I'm sure her fiancée had something to do with it."

"What is his name?"

"Bradley Turner."

"No," I could hear Stephanie mumbling as the paramedic whisked her past.

"I have to go with her," I anxiously told the officer.

"Do you know where he is?" he questioned.

"No, he wasn't here when I got here. Please I have to be with her."

"Okay," the officer replied allowing me to walk by and catch up with the paramedic.

As I followed the ambulance to the hospital I regretted telling Miss Pearl what happened in that way. I worried that she may get in an accident and I immediately called her to see if she needed me to pick her up on the way. Thankfully her neighbor was bringing her and they were almost there.

Once at the hospital, the paramedics rushed Stephanie inside and doctors took her into one of the emergency rooms. Miss Pearl arrived while I waited in the family room. A long half hour later, the doctor came out and reported on her condition. Thankfully, she only suffered a mild concussion. We went to see her in her room and she looked a lot better than the grotesque scene back at the house. She was sitting upright in the bed, bandage on her head, and ice on her lip. It hurt to see her in pain. Looking at her was almost like looking at a mirror of my past. All doubts of whether to call off the divorce where out the window.

"Oh baby," Miss pearl sobbed as she went to sit by her. I joined them and we sat there together, no words necessary. Not long after we settled in the room, the same police officer that came up to me at the house entered the room. He offered his sympathy and then moved forward with his investigation of her attack.

"Rest assured, we have Bradley in custody, but we still need to go over the details of what happened," he stated.

"Wait," Stephanie argued, "you have to let him go."

"You can't protect him, honey," I warned.

"Why is he in custody," she asked, ignoring my comment.

"He has to pay for his actions," I responded, cutting off the officer. "I was afraid that something like this would happen. I'm just glad it wasn't worse."

"That's right," Miss Pearl added and reached for her daughter's hand. Stephanie quickly pulled her hand away.

"You all aren't listening. Brad did not do this; I don't know why you arrested him. He wasn't even home when it happened,"

Stephanie disputed. The officer fumbled with his notepad and looked around the room at each of our faces confused.

"Ma'am, we had to pick him up once we were told about the altercation between you two. Please tell me what happened."

"There was no altercation between Brad and I; why aren't you listening to me," Stephanie pleaded.

"The bruises on your face tell another story," I continued, "trust me I know what it is like to be in your situation."

"No you don't!" she yelled, "You told them he did this," she asked, furiously looking at me.

"Yes, I cannot stand by and watch him do this to you," I replied.

"Tammy, you need to leave," she sternly stated.

"Ladies, let's calm down," the officer interjected. "Please Stephanie, tell me what happened."

"Bradley left because Jonathan Sr. was coming to pick up J.B.," she said rolling her eyes at me, "when he got to the house I could tell he had been drinking. I told him he could not take J.B. with him and he got upset and we argued. He picked up my vase off the table and hit me with it. When I came to, I was being hauled off to the hospital."

The information shocked me and I was frozen in place. I couldn't express to her how bad I felt.

"What is Jonathan's full name," the officer asked.

"Please, you have to get my son back," she cried.

The officer got the information on J.B's father and I stood there unable to utter a word. Miss Pearl coddled her daughter and I just stood there.

"Stephanie, I'm so sorry," I finally said.

"Please just leave," she told me.

"Stephanie," I tried to plead.

"No, just leave. Look I know you went through a lot with your husband but your meddling has gone too far. You need to go."

I wanted to comfort her and be there for her, but I respected her wishes.

Alexis

Once we got back to the apartment after leaving the hospital, I went straight to my room to find the number I jotted down from the game. Sure enough it was Isaiah calling Eugene. The idea that they knew each other took me for a spin. I couldn't think of a plausible scenario that made sense or that made me feel better about it. I held on to the information and decided to ignore both of them until I figured out what to do. Kina went to bed as soon as we got home and I left her to rest. I figured we could talk soon enough.

The next morning I had to go to the office of WSJ, and Kina was still resting when I left. I was nervous about running into Eugene because I wasn't sure how I was going to play my hand. I rushed to my cubicle and pulled out the assignment I was supposed to be working on. Then I started my investigation of Eugene. I nonchalantly asked Jessica, a journalist, what she thought about Eugene. She seemed down to earth and in the know.
"Eugene, the investigative reporter," she asked with a light chuckle.
"No, the sports writer," I corrected her.

"Yeah, he has a sports column but he started as an investigative reporter and some of his best work deals with his news coverage."

"Really," I replied playfully hoping she would continue.

"Yes, but he is hard to get close to. Believe me I've tried several times," she said nudging me in the arm as if we were the best of friends. "Why do you ask?"

"I was just curious. He always seems to himself," I lied building off her description of him.

"You're right about that. But don't worry he won't bite," she replied and turned to leave. She promised to talk to me later but I didn't count on it.

I immediately went back to my desk and started looking at some of the articles he's written in the past. Nothing jumped out at me and I wondered why he never mentioned this side of his career before. Maybe he thought that being a sports writer made him more attractive, I thought. Just as I was about to write off the omission, I came across an article about the Stevenson trial. Obviously Max Stevenson was facing some serious charges for drug trafficking and distribution. An officer was working undercover for months hoping to infiltrate the group and bring him down. The case was making progress but when the FDA set up a sting, the operation went bad. The undercover officer was suspected of turning and disappeared. The gang that was supposed to make the deal with

Stevenson's team, the Rack Squad, disappeared as well. Only one of the member of the rival gang was found, beaten and not willing to talk. When I read the name of the gang, I lost the ability to breathe. They were called the Suffolk Street Mafia or S.S.M. That was the gang that my ex Dante was involved with, and who almost cost me my life. Dante seemed like the perfect boyfriend. I was hopelessly in love and carelessly did a run for him. I remember when he asked me to take something to his friend for him.

"Why, what is it," I asked confused by his request.

"You ask too many questions," he said with a smile, kissing me on the cheek trying to minimize my suspicion.

"Maybe I'm not asking enough," I replied pulling away.

"Babe, can we talk about this after you get back," he asked still with a smile on his face.

"Why can't you take it?"

"Because I need to meet up with Q. Look baby you're making a big deal out of nothing," he assured me pulling me closer to him. "I would take it myself but Q is in a bind right now. I wouldn't ask you if I didn't think it was safe. Don't you trust me?" He asked pulling away from me enough to look me in my eyes. Anger burned inside my stomach and something told me to say no. I should have. To this day, I can still hear him saying those words, 'don't you trust me.' Despite my instinct I agreed to go this once and that we would have a talk when we both returned. I got the address from him and took my car to the Suffolk projects. While en route to my destination I called Kina and explained the situation I allowed myself to get into. She urged me to take it back to Dante and leave him, but I couldn't. I promised her that after this I was done. The house looked abandoned and I stood out by my car. My doubts increased so I got back in my car and called Dante.

"What do you mean you can't do it?" he asked. I could hear traffic in the background so I knew he must be out the house already.

"It just doesn't feel right. Can't you just meet me here…"

"I already told you I need to meet Q. Baby please just go inside and drop it off and come straight home. I really need you to help me out."

"Okay," I replied.

"I love you…" he returned but I hung up not wanting to hear his voice any longer. I took in a deep breath to get myself together. I put my phone in my pocket and grabbed the pack from my back seat. By the time I made my way up the stairs to the door it was opened. A guy pulled me inside. It wasn't hard but enough to raise my alarm.

"I'm just dropping this off for Dante," I stated firmly but inside I trembled with anxiety. There were three guys inside. All of them looked dangerous so I handed it to the man closest to me and he handed it to a dark-skinned guy that was sitting. He stood up and I could tell by his expensive clothes, compared to the others, that he must've been in charge. Not wanting to spend any more time in the same room with them, I quickly turned to leave.

"Wait a minute, Lil Mama, I have to check this out first. Everything in here," he asked holding the pack up. He smiled at me but nothing about him gave off a positive energy.

"I honestly don't even know what it is," I replied. It was then that the gravity of my error in coming here sunk in. I felt stupid for agreeing to bring an unopened package to someone I never met before. No matter what it was I knew it couldn't be good. He never opened the package. He had one of his thugs bring him a scale and I assumed it was drugs. He laughed in disbelief; obviously it didn't weigh what it should. Again I turned to leave but the man by the door prevented me from leaving.

"Please, I just want to go home. I don't have anything to do with this," I begged fighting the tears in my eyes.

"You are very much involved," he replied coming closer to me. He reached for my purse and I let him have it.

"Relax, I'm not going to hurt you. I just want assurance that Dante will give me what he owes me," he fumbled through my purse and found my wallet and took out my license.

I stood there unable to move, unable to speak.

"I'm really a nice guy," he continued, "I could have kidnapped you, killed you. But I'm a sucker for pretty girls. I'm Rugga, by the way."

He held out his hand for me to shake but I declined. He gave me my purse back, keeping the license.

"You tell Dante to come see me, okay," he stated as if this was a normal, professional interaction. "Otherwise, things are going to get real political."

I shook my head in agreement thankful he was letting me go.

"Hey stranger," Eugene said peeping in my cubicle causing me to gasp.

I minimized the screen and turned to face him.

"Hi," I quickly responded hoping my over eagerness and high pitched tone didn't seem suspicious.

"You haven't been returning my calls."

"I know; I'm sorry. I've been really busy. I have a lot on my plate right now" I replied feigning drowsiness. I could feel a drop of sweat roll down my back but I tried to appear normal.

"Well maybe we can talk about it over lunch," he proposed.

"I can't. I have a lot to catch up on," I lied.

"Dinner then?"

"I can't," I replied gathering my things together so that I could leave.

"Are you sure you're okay?" he asked with his eyebrows raised.

"Yeah, I'm fine. I just have to work," I again lied, "I'll call you though."

Immediately I called Kina and her phone went straight to voicemail. I headed to the apartment to check on her, and to piece the information I found out at work with what Kina knows about him. After all, it was her idea that I date Eugene in the first place.

When I walked into the apartment, I could tell she had done some cleaning, which was a good sign that she was feeling better. I checked her bedroom and she wasn't there. Once I realized she wasn't in the apartment, I glanced out the window to see if her car was outside. Her car was in her parking space so I tried calling her again. Once more I got her voicemail. I left her a message to call me as soon as possible and went to do some more research on articles Eugene wrote about SSM and the Stevenson trial.

Sherri

I was an empty shell at work. It was if I was operating on auto pilot. My sister's memory has not improved and her IQ level seems as if it has dropped. Scans of her brain still shows swelling and I felt so overwhelmed. Tammy keeps calling me but I just can't get over the fact that she and everyone else knew what was happening with Kina and Tyler and she didn't tell me.

On the way home I picked the children up from daycare and stopped for takeout. Terra and Michelle ate in front of the television and I sat Derrick in his high chair.

While I changed my clothes I heard the front door and the girls laughing.

"I know you did not just answer the door," I scorned as I went to investigate.

"It's just Aunt Tammy," Terra explained.

"I don't care, you still ask me before you open the door. What if it was a stranger?"

She shrugged her shoulders and then she and her sister scurried off into her room. Tammy just stood at the door silent.

"What are you doing here?" I finally asked.

"We should talk. I've been trying to reach you."

She made her way into the living room without invitation but I didn't stop her.

"I don't know if I'm ready to talk to you yet," I held my ground.

"And why not," she asked, "what is your problem?"

"You know my problem."

"Actually, I don't. I'm not the one who hurt you and I consider myself a good friend. What changed?"

"If you were such a good friend, why didn't you tell me about Kina and Tyler?"

"I wanted to give Kina the opportunity to come clean, and I didn't realize it had gotten so deep. I love you Sherri, like a sister. Don't let that fade," she pleaded tears falling.

I realized that I had been crying as well. "I miss you," I replied giving in to the embrace she offered. I didn't realize how much I missed her company until then.

"Things have been really hard," I admitted.

"I'm here for you."

I sat back in the chair and started to pour out all the emotion I had been holding in.

"My mom keeps pushing me to forgive Tyler and Kina and it hurts because I actually miss him."

"Oh Sherri, I know how it feels to be betrayed by someone you love so deeply. Just don't rush to make a decision. Forgiving doesn't always mean running back."

"Can you believe I called him and he hasn't called me back or anything?"

Just saying the words caused me to cry again. She hugged me once more and when she let go I could see that she was crying too.

"Forgive and let him go," she advised. "Have you spoken to Kina?"

"Don't even bring her up. I'm done with her."

"She messed up. Heck I'm mad at her too but…"

"But nothing," I stopped her.

"Don't you want to know what 'problems' Tyler is supposedly having?"

"Not if it means talking to her or Alexis?"

"Would you at least be open to talking to Alexis sometime? I know she said some things to hurt you, but it was out of anger and I know she cares about you."

"I don't know. It's funny, I defended her to that Detective but I can't bring myself to forgive her for throwing out my personal information and siding with 'Judas.'"

"Why is a detective interested in her?" Tammy asked shocked by the information.

"Myers came by the hospital and asked if I thought she knew about Renee's attack and mentioned that her family has been under surveillance. For what, I don't know."

"You don't think it has anything to do with Lex's boys roughing up those drug dealers back in college?"

"I honestly don't know. I doubt it though."

"Still, maybe we should let her know."

"You can but I'm still not talking to her right now."

Kina

When I walked into my apartment, Alexis was in the dining room on her laptop. I thought I could slide past her without notice, but she caught me.

"I was worried about you," she said.

She came over to me and gave me a strong hug.

"I'm sorry. I guess I should have left a note or something."

"Yes, trick, you should have," she joked, "especially with all the drama that's been going on lately."

"True. I'll be right back," I conceded and went to put my bag down in my room.

I debated if I should be upfront about my little disappearing act. The stress I have been going through is weighing on me but I know that everyone is still angry about Tyler. Alexis is still talking to me and I don't want to ruin that with the truth.

"So why aren't you at The Journal," I asked once I returned to the dining room. Her look was one I've seen before and it alarmed me.

"What is it?"

"What do you know about Eugene?"

"Nothing bad, otherwise I wouldn't have vouched for him. What did he do?"

I took a seat next to her at the table.

"Nothing exactly," she responded and I waited for her to continue. "Strike one was the females, he always seemed so into me, but you know what I overheard at his place. I was able to let that go but at the game I peeped his phone and Isaiah was calling him."

"For what?" I asked shockingly.

"I don't know. He was at the concession stand and I didn't answer it. Anyway, did you know he is an investigative reporter?"

"Yeah, so," I replied not sure why it mattered.

"Well he never mentioned it to me. He just introduced himself as a sports writer. When I found out, I did some research on his work and he wrote some articles about Max Stevenson and a gang he was associated with," she paused for emphasis, "The S.S.M"

"No," I replied in disbelief, "but that doesn't necessarily mean anything."

I hoped to calm my anxiety as much as hers.

"Or it could mean everything. Didn't you say he asked about me?"

"Yes, but that doesn't necessarily mean he knows you are involved. Besides if he or the police knew Lex's team had anything to do with taking out S.S.M. they wouldn't have waited years to do anything about it."

"Maybe you're right, but what about Isaiah? Do you think they are running some kind of game?"

"I doubt it… I don't know. Maybe you should just ask him."

"Maybe. It just all seems suspicious."

"Okay Sherlock, just don't go all DEFCON 3 on him. It may all be innocent and Eugene seems like a nice guy that is really digging you. Just in case…"

"I'll tread lightly, but you have to be my Watson on this," she continued the joke and I laughed. "Anyway, where were you today," she asked suspiciously.

"You love me no matter what right…"

"Yes…" she replied cautiously.

"I was with Tyler," I paused to try and read her. She shrugged her shoulders and shook her head as if she already knew. "It's not what you think," I continued, "he wanted to talk and I agreed to meet him. When they were working on each other at school for an assignment, Tyler found out he has an irregular heartbeat."

"Wow. Is he okay?"

"It's nothing significant so far, just something they will have to monitor. Anyway he hadn't told anybody and I know he was anxious about it and very depressed. I know it was wrong to meet up with him again but I felt like I at least should be there for him."

"Babe you don't owe him anything. I know it's rough for him right now, but like you said, it's not life or death."

"You're right. I just feel bad. He could have at least talked to Sherri if it wasn't for me."

"You messed up, but he is just as responsible. If he wanted to talk to Sherri he could have done that instead of getting involved with you, no offense."

"None taken. Anyway, he's okay. He wants us to try a relationship but I just can't," I started to cry. I was so firm when I turned him down, but speaking to Alexis I couldn't hide my true emotions. She put her hand on mine and let me continue.

"I feel bad for him, and for Sherri. The truth is I am so upset about my decision and I would delete him from my life permanently if I could."

"You can, I'm here for you no matter what."

"Good, because I'm pregnant," I confided.

"No," she said shocked. "I thought it only happened once."

"It only takes one time," I replied embarrassed that I let this happen.

"Does he know?"

"No. I found out from the doctor today. I don't know what to do," I told her.

Tammy

After being at work all day, all I could think about was crashing on the sofa. When Rod and I got home Janise was again on the telephone. I realized that our days consist of school, work, take out, television and no time together. Even though the couch was calling me, I decided to cook in and get Janise to help me.
"Am I being punished for something?" Janise asked once I informed her of my plans.
"What, no. We need to spend more time together. I feel like we don't even know each other anymore."
"Why!" she protested, "I'm the same person. Besides I'm supposed to call Nicole back in twenty minutes once she's off the phone with Kim and after I text Kayla."
"You can either cut your phone off for the rest of the day and spend time with your family, or I can take it for the rest of the week. Your choice."
"The rest of the evening! This really sounds like punishment, mom. Can't we do this another time."
"Is spending time with your family that bad," I asked upset at how out of pocket Janise has become.
She marched off toward her bedroom.
"Janise Marie James," I called behind her.

"I'm putting my phone on the charger," she snapped not turning around.

"Watch it," I threatened.

Dinner preparations did not go as well as I hoped. Rod enjoyed helping from beginning to end but Janise gave me grief from the moment she came out of her room. I don't know when my little girl was swapped for this little vampire that I don't recognize. Rod and I focused on the lasagna layering and tried to ignore Janise's lack of enthusiasm. My plan for bonding was backfiring and several times I thought of just sending Janise to her room. I stuck it out and a couple of times I could have sworn she was enjoying herself but when I pointed it out she closed back up again.

While the lasagna was baking in the oven Sherri stopped by. She was dressed well but I could tell that the drama was taking a toll on her.

"Will you be able to stay for dinner," Rod asked enthusiastically.

"You bet," she replied with a smile.

"You guys can go hang out in the den or in your bedrooms," I said.

Rod ran off and Janise just stood in the entrance to the living room.

"Is there a problem," I asked.

"Nothing," she said and stormed off.

"Is that what I have to look forward to," Sherri rhetorically asked.

"It comes with the territory. How are you holding up?"

"As best I can. I just needed a moment away. It hurts to be around Renee and she's not improving as much as I'd like and her kids are a constant reminder of what's going on," she grumbled.

"Well, you can't let that get you down; the doctor said it would take time. Besides, think of how far she's come along."

"I guess you're right. I just can't help but think that one day I'm going to wake up and it's just me and the kids," she said with a sniffle.

"You can't think like that. You have to be optimistic for her and especially the children."

"Who is going to be that for me?"

"I'm here for you."

"Thanks," she replied.

Sometimes I want to snatch Sherri up and tell her to pull it together but I know she responds better to coddling. I just hope she doesn't sink herself into depression while wallowing in her sister's sorrow.

"Have you talked to Alexis," I asked.

"No," she responded dramatically. "Have you?"

"No, but I think we should. Now we need each other more than ever."

"You do whatever you want to do," she replied swapping her sadness for resentment.

"Can't you at least do a dinner with the three of us so we can talk?"

"Not as long as she's siding with her," she snapped.

"I don't think it's a matter of sides. You can't take Kina's mistake out on her. Don't you think our friendship is at least worth a dinner?"

"I don't know. All I know is the trust has been broken…"

"All the more room for improvement," I interrupted.

"I'm not making any promises."

Chapter 11

Alexis

It was time for Sunday dinner at my mom's. Surprisingly I hadn't talked to Lex or Trina since the incident. The situation with Eugene piqued my curiosity even further about my Dad's business but I knew Lex would be tight with the information, especially around Mama. And I couldn't exactly milk my source, Missy, with her being in custody and my anger still brewing.

"It's about time you showed up, dinner is getting cold," my mom greeted as I walked into her place.

"I'm sorry, I got caught up at Glam. You should've started without me," I responded even though I know Mama has a thing about eating together as a family. Even when it was just the two of us she made sure we sat together at the table.

"Well go wash up. Lex and Trina are already in the dining room."

"How are things at work?" Lex asked me once I took a seat at the table. The baby was asleep in her carrier next to Trina.

"Okay. They finally cleared everything up but I'm not getting promoted anytime soon," I replied.

"I'm sorry to hear that," Mama added.

"I'm not. I've got my hands full at The Journal."

"Any interesting stories?" Trina inquired.

"Not really, just a lot of busy work." I chose to keep my new discoveries at bay until I figured out the best way to approach Lex about it.

"How is your cousin doing; is she out of the hospital yet?" Mama asked.

"I don't know and I really don't care." I replied.

The tension eased over dinner and I wondered if I could confront Lex about what was going on. I decided to wait until I got more information. I received calls from both Isaiah and Eugene but I didn't want to speak to either of them until I got to the bottom of things.

When I got to Kina's apartment, things were quiet. Ever since the attack I have been anxious about entering silent apartments. I finished my sweep through and I realized all was normal. There was a note from Kina that she would be home later. I sighed at the thought that she could be with Tyler. I decided to withhold my judgments. Besides I'm caught up in my own life right now and no matter what I think about Kina's actions, she is my sister and she has a good heart.

On my laptop, I continued my investigation of my love life and the Stevenson case. I came across some more articles about the rogue undercover cop. One of them had a picture of Isaiah. I opened the article and read on. Isaiah Harris was a detective. He told me his last name was Jefferson, but looking at the picture, I'm sure this was him. My heart sank and I thought about every encounter with him. This would explain why I could never drop my guard around him and why he seemed so eager. Still, I don't understand what he wants with me. Just as I was contemplating, Kina walked in.

"You don't look so hot," she stated as she took a seat next to me at the dining room table.

"I could say the same," I responded noticing how troubled and disheveled she looked despite her designer outfit and make-up. She remained silent. I stared at her hoping she would tell me where she's been or what she's thinking. She just gave a halfhearted smile.

"Anyway," I continued, "I found out some information about Isaiah."

"Great, I could use a distraction right now. Besides you had me worrying about you."

"Well the undercover cop that was suspected of turning that went missing is Isaiah..."

"No!" she exclaimed. "What does he want with you? Did he ask anything about college?"

"Never, well, not really. He always asked about my time in college and friends that I made but I thought he was just trying to get to know me. It always seemed forced; and now I know why."

"I still don't understand why he would be interested in you. Didn't you say he was investigating someone named Max Stevenson? Have you even heard of that name before?"

"No, but from what I've read so far he was supposed to be making some drug deal and then the deal went bad, some people died, some went missing. I wonder if Dante's crew was involved and if that's why they are interested in me?"

"Even so, how would the police know you were involved with Dante? Maybe it's all just a coincidence," Kina tried to assure me.

"I hope so," I replied wanting to believe her. But why would he be calling Eugene? And could I trust Eugene? Unlike Isaiah, he seemed genuine. Now I don't know what to believe.

"Maybe you should talk to Eugene." Kina suggested.

"Not until I know more. So where have you been?"

"I was going to talk to Tyler but I remembered what you said at the hospital about Sherri and how he didn't want kids. Plus, I feel bad about this whole situation. I ended up at the frozen yogurt place and I just sat in the parking lot crying, and thinking."

"You should have called me," I retorted.

"I know, I just needed to be alone. I know you are here for me, but don't pretend like you aren't disappointed."

"Well yeah, but that doesn't mean I don't care about you. We all make mistakes, and while I hate that it is Tyler, I'm not judging you. What's done is done and all we can do is try to move on. Thicker than blood, remember," I assured her grabbing her hand from across the table.

"Thank you," she said stifling tears. "So," she continued attempting to pull herself together, "we have to get to the bottom of this Isaiah thing. I'll grab my laptop and we can investigate together."

Sherri

My routine has become back to normal, if that still exists. I have been busy at work and I've found an apartment to accommodate the kids. Still my mom is keeping them most of the time. Tammy has been calling me constantly. Truthfully, I've been taking on more work so I don't have to face her or any of my so called friends. I want to take my mom's advice and try and forgive and move on, but some hurtful things were said, secrets were kept, and I don't know who to trust anymore. My sorority sisters have caused me to doubt everything I know about love and friendship. Tammy holding out on me hurts the most. Since college she has always been like the mentor to us. Even though she wasn't our sorority sister, she became our 'sister.' Still, she has been in my corner since everything went down and hasn't had any judgment about my abortion despite how strongly she feels about it. Yet I can't seem to answer her calls or anyone's. Tyler has always been my rock and now he won't even answer my calls. When did everything change between us? I knew we were going through a rough patch, but I never thought it was this deep. I rummaged the apartment for dinner and turned up empty. Luckily for me Tammy showed up bearing take out.

"How have you been holding up," Tammy inquired.

"Better now that Renee has been moved to the rehab facility. Things are looking good for her. Still, we are taking it one day at a time."

"I'm glad to hear it. Look I know that things have been stressed between us but know that I never did anything to intentionally hurt you and I'm here for you, always will be."

"Thank you. I admit that it is hard for me to trust anyone but I know that you have my best interest at heart and I'm glad to call you my friend. I'm ready to move on."

"So when can we get up with the rest of the gang?"

"Don't push it. I'm moving on, but that doesn't mean I want to spend any time with them right now."

"We have to address it sometime. I know we all made mistakes in this situation but we have always been there for each other and we need the support from each other. Especially now."

"That's easier said than done. I don't know if I can ever face Kina again. And you know Alexis is siding with her, plus she said some nasty things when she laid all my business out."

"Yes but we can't hold onto that forever…"

"Whatever," I interrupted, "I'm glad you're here but if you are going to spend the whole time talking about them I'd rather be alone."

Tammy

After I left Sherri's I headed back to an empty house. The kids were again with their father and I cut the evening with Sherri short. I'm glad that we could work things out but I want things to get back to normal with all of us. Everything seems broken. My heart is crushed because the love of my life turned on me and I don't know if I can ever trust him again. He has been doing great with the kids but I just can't let him back in. I was so torn and hurt when I signed the divorce papers, but deep down I know that I made the right choice.

I tried to get Stephanie on the phone but she didn't answer. I apologized to her, and she says she's over it, but things still aren't the same between us. I was happy that J.B. is now with her full time but she is so lost in her fiancée right now. I'm glad that I was wrong about him. Still, I feel like it is too soon for them to marry. Just as I was about to conclude that she was avoiding me, I heard my doorbell.

"Sorry to drop by so late," Stephanie greeted.

"No, I'm glad to see you; I just tried to call."

"I know. I was on the phone with Brad. Since I was in the area, I decided to come see you in person."

"Well how have you been?" I asked as we settled into my living room. Her beauty was not marred by damage done by Jonathan Sr. She has the incision on her head covered well with foundation.

"Better. Brad and I have set a date for the wedding and have even found a house to buy. It looks like we are finally going to be a family."

"I'm happy for you."

"Are you really," she asked, aware of my constant objections to her rush.

"Yes," I honestly replied. "I think it's too soon, but who am I to rain on your parade? I wish the best for you."

"Thank you. Now we can talk about wedding plans, I want you to be my maid of honor."

We stayed up late talking about wedding plans and life. I was happy that one of my friendships seemed genuinely repaired. I chose not to break out the wine to celebrate. After Alexis' comments I have really been cutting back.

That Sunday I was awakened by a wide eyed Rod hopping on my bed. I embraced him glad that they were back home. We walked downstairs to greet Janise and to tell Kenny goodbye. Janise was in the family room flipping through the channels.

"Did Dad leave already," Rod asked.

"Yes," Janise replied shortly.

"Aww man, I didn't get to say goodbye" Rod whined.

"How was your weekend," I asked Janise.

"Fine," she replied not even looking up at me.

"Janise Marie, you could at least look at me when I'm talking to you."

She abruptly turned her attention to me, irritation covering her face. My mom would have never accepted this kind of behavior.

"What has gotten into you?" I demanded.

"Nothing, it's not like you care anyway!" she yelled.

"Excuse me, since when do you use that tone with your mother!"

She got up to leave and Rod stood there wide eyed looking as if he was afraid of being in trouble by association.

"You get back here; Roderick, go to your room for a minute."

"Yes ma'am," he responded as if grateful for the exit.

"What," Janise asked with too much attitude.

"Little girl, you need to bring it down a notch. What is going on with you? Since when am I the enemy"

"Since you neglected us for your friends. You say you love us and want to spend time with us, but you are always at work or with your friends."

I stood there shocked; mostly from her response then the sass that came with it.

"I do love you. And, yes, I have been busy, but that is no excuse for you to be disrespectful" I said sternly. Then my demeanor softened as she broke out in tears. I took her into my arms and she broke free.

"If you love us so much, why do you keep trying to send us over to dad's just to get rid of us. I remember the bad things he did to you. Why do you care about being with your friends so much that you are choosing them over us?"

"That is not true," I replied feeling hurt that she felt that way.

"Then why did you say you want family night and as soon as Aunt Sherri showed up you sent us to our rooms?'

"I'm sorry. I was so focused on what your aunt Sherri was going through that I didn't think about how it would make you feel. I didn't mean to hurt you, you and Rod mean the most to me and nothing or no one can come between us."

Tears fell from her eyes and I went to hold her again. This time she let me embrace her and we stood there, mending the broken bond between daughter and mother.

Kina

Nervousness rushed through my veins as I sat behind my desk at The Journal. The whole day I succeeded in avoiding Eugene, but as I sat here investigating for Alexis I felt vulnerable. I decided to tap into the company's database to see if there were any articles about the Stevenson case or Isaiah that didn't make it to print. The search turned up an article written by Eugene that was half finished but there weren't any notes or much information. From what I could gather, he was writing an article about the possibility of Isaiah being innocent of the shooting and who the drug deal was supposed to be with; the SSM, just as Alexis had suspected. There wasn't anything about Alexis or Dante. There was someone named Quinton Graham who was there but he never showed up for his court date and was at large. Apparently, Isaiah stated that Quinton was the key to proving what really happened that night. Nothing else of interest popped up, so I printed what I found and left to find Alexis.

When I discovered that Alexis was not at her desk, I called her to and found out that she was already at my place.
"I have news," I declared as I rushed through the foyer and to the dining area where Alexis was sitting in front of her laptop.

"What's up?" Alexis asked looking up from the screen. I sat next to her and laid out the articles I printed.

"Well, it looks like Eugene was writing about Isaiah and him possibly being innocent, and how finding one of the dealers name Quinton was supposed to help prove everything but then he disappeared," I blurted out, half rambling with excitement. Alexis sat there in awe as if she were taking it all in.

"So, Isaiah is Eugene's source," she broke the silence, "so they both have been using me to get to information about Dante and his people."

"We don't know that for sure. Just because Eugene wrote some articles about what happened, doesn't mean that he has linked you to anything."

"If so, why has he been in touch with Isaiah recently? And the name Quinton, I wonder if that was the guy named Q that Dante was supposed to meet that day he had me make his run."

"Maybe," I replied. "I don't like this. If Eugene thinks you are involved, why wouldn't he just ask you?"

"That's what I want to know. And he seemed so genuine. I think now all there is to do is just confront him about the articles and Isaiah."

"Have you let your brother in on what you found out?"

"Not yet, I will tell him after I talk to Eugene."

She called him on the phone and arranged to meet him for dinner. That left me to decide whether or not to let Tyler in on the pregnancy. Fear of rejection, fear of having to face an abortion like Sherri, suffering the guilt of it, facing the shame from Alexis, all are reasons why I don't want to call. Yet I still felt like he should know. I mustered up the courage and called.

"I'm surprised to hear from you," he spoke.

"Yeah me too. I need to talk to you."

"Do you want me to come over?"

"No," I said abruptly. It was hard enough to talk to him over the phone. Plus, I didn't want to risk him running into Alexis. "I just wanted to let you know that I'm pregnant. I don't expect anything; I just thought you should know."

"Wait, what? I thought you were on birth control."

"No, I'm not. I mentioned that before, but your mind was obviously on something else."

"So you're saying this is my fault?" he exclaimed.

"No, we both are responsible. And there is no use placing blame, what's done is done. Like I said, I'm not asking you for anything, I just thought you should know. And I'm keeping the baby."

"Wow, I don't know what to say. I mean I'm still in Med School, and this all just happened so fast."

"Don't say anything. Anyway, now you know. I have to go."

I hung up the phone before he could respond. I don't know how I expected him to react but I guess it could have been worse. And I don't know how to face Sherri and Tammy now that I have a baby by Tyler. Especially, since Sherri gave up hers. Sherri probably will never speak to me again after what happened anyway. Still the loss hurts. We may not have been as close as Alexis and I, but she still was a good friend most of the time. Also, I don't want Tammy to be disappointed in me. I guess now it's too late.

Alexis

Eugene walked in and had a seat across from me. We chose to meet at the diner he took me to for lunch. I didn't know if I could trust Eugene, so I had him meet me in a public place. As I sat across from him, his smile was charming. I still felt uneasy. Suddenly, I regretted not talking to my brother beforehand. The waiter came and took our drink orders.

"I'm glad you finally got in touch with me. Is everything okay?"

"Not really," I answered, not sure of how to begin. He gave me his full attention and as I looked into his eyes I felt as if I could be honest. "I was looking at some of you old articles and I noticed that you did a story on someone I used to date, Isaiah," I paused noticing his recognition but he didn't say anything so I continued. "He's the one who wrote the note that I lost. Anyway, from your article I found out that he was a cop. Is that why you asked me out?"

"No," he replied sternly. I wanted to believe him but I couldn't just yet. "You're right, I did write some articles about one of his cases, but I didn't know you were involved when I met you."

"And you think I'm involved, now," I asked irritated.

"I don't know."

"Why didn't you just ask me? How can I trust this isn't some game? Obviously, Isaiah has been playing me from the jump. How do I know you weren't setting me up all along?"

"Look," he said reaching for my hand but I pulled it away. I could feel the anger burning in my face, surprised at how emotional this was getting me. "Isaiah reached out to me after he saw you with me. I didn't know he was following you for his case."

"Following me, so not only has he been trying to deceive me, you're telling me he has been following me," I exclaimed as hushed as I could. The waiter came to ask if everything was okay and took our empty glasses away.

"I'm ready for the check," Eugene said to the waiter then returned his attention to me. "When I asked you out, I had no idea that you were involved in this case."

"I'm not involved in anything!" I denied. "I don't know what he's told you, but I had nothing to do with his case and I don't want to have anything to do with you."

I stormed out of the diner and searched for my keys. Before I could drive away, he walked behind my car. Despite how mad I was, I couldn't run him over. So, I got out to tell him to move.

"Listen to me," Eugene pleaded. "You're right; I should have been up front with you about what I found out."

"There is nothing to find out," I argued, "I told you I had nothing to do with that." At least that was mostly true.

"So you weren't dating one of the drug dealers?" He asked knowingly.

"Look don't judge me," I replied angrily and started to leave again.

"I'm not judging you," he responded, pulling me closer to face him. "If you say you weren't involved I believe you. I heard his version now I want to hear from you."

"Now you want to know," I asked upset at how good he was at disarming me, especially since I didn't know if I could trust him yet.

"Yes."

I stood there trying not to get lost in his eyes again.

"I dated this guy named Dante in college. I didn't realize what he was into until it was too late. I ended things immediately after I found out. I don't know anything else," I told him. This was mostly true. I don't know how my brother handled things when Rugga started threatening me after Dante disappeared. All I know is none of them ever contacted me again. I don't ask questions I don't want to know the answers to.

"Okay," he said, satisfied with my response.

"Okay," I repeated. I wanted to be closer to him, to let him comfort me but I couldn't. I pulled away and got in my car. I needed to get away from him and clear my head.

"Call me, I don't think Isaiah is a dirty cop, but I still don't trust him around you," he mentioned as he held my door. I started my car.

"I thought you two were friends," I probed.

"Professionally, he seems like a good cop caught up with some bad people. But even good cops get eccentric when they feel they have nothing to lose."

"Fine," I agreed not sure if I would keep the promise. He closed my door and I drove away.

Sherri

The days seemed to go by monotonously. My sister is doing well but she still has to stay for physical therapy. She recognizes her children and seems to be fine outside of the mood swings. Damage to her leg has her in need of crutches but the doctors can't risk her falling until her brain has healed more. After dutifully spending the evening with her I went to my parents' house to pick up the kids. My mom has a doctor's appointment in the morning so I have to take the kids to school and daycare before work.

"Hi daddy, Mommy," I greeted my parents as I approached them as they were sitting in the living room watching Law and Order. "Sorry I'm late."

"I'll go get the kids out of bed," my mom offered.

I sat down next to my father.

"Do you think I'm selfish," I asked him.

"Why do you ask," he responded finally turning from the screen. A commercial was on.

"Well, one of the girls said that I'm self-absorbed. And I've been thinking, maybe that's why Tyler lost interest or why I didn't notice he was drifting away," I said softly, determined not to cry again. Not in front of Daddy. Suddenly, I had his full attention. Winning against the SVU.

"Baby, what happened isn't your fault," he said putting his arm around me. "You can be demanding, but I raised you that way; you deserve the best. Now, what happened between your friends isn't on you. Everybody has a choice, and sometimes we make the wrong ones. It's their loss," he said, kissing me on the forehead. Then we both sat back and watched the show until mom came back down stairs with the kids following behind her.

After I put the kids to bed I called Tammy.
"What's going on," Tammy said in a whisper.
"Nothing much, I didn't wake you did I?"
"No I'm reading. Rod had a nightmare so he is asleep next to me. Let me put him to bed."
She muted the phone and in a few minutes returned.
"Is everything all right?" she asked.
"Yeah, I was just replaying how things went down. Do you think I could have done anything differently?"
There was a long pause before she answered.
"I think nothing you did could have justified what happened. We all go through things but it's no excuse to sleep with someone behind your back. Still, I think that Kina truly didn't mean for it to happen."
"Well it did," I exclaimed, my anger rising again. "I don't want to talk about her, I meant my relationship with Tyler. We have been

friends since I was 12, how could I not see that my best friend was slipping away. I mean, am I that self-absorbed."

I felt the warmth of my tears decorating my face. I didn't bother to wipe them.

"People change, he isn't the same person he was 10 years ago, none of us are. Who knew it would end like this?"

"But I didn't want it to end. I mean he messed up, and forgiving him is hard but I still love him. We have history; how can he just throw all of that away. He's not even answering my calls," I confided, my silent tears now turning into ugly sobs.

"Honey, it's messed up, I know but you can't change what happened or how he feels. Who knows how long he has been holding back his true feelings. All you can do know is try to move on. You are young, beautiful, and successful. This is the end of your relationship, not the end of you."

"I know, it's just hard."

"It is, but you have your family and you know I'm here for you. Your friends can be too if we try to smooth things out. We have history with them too."

"I feel bad about what happened with me and Alexis," I admitted "She didn't deserve all my anger but I was emotional and it's hard to reach out to her knowing she is still friends with Kina. Uhh"

I heard Tammy sigh.

"Well, as messed up as she is, she needs a friend too."

"Well it won't be me. I may speak to Alexis one day but Kina, hmm never. That friendship was annulled the minute she nailed my boyfriend."

Tammy

Since Janise bared her true feelings, I have been making more of an effort to spend time with the kids. Although she still has the teenage attitude, she is making the effort. Stephanie and I took the kids to the arcade. Even though Janise insists that she wants more family time, she seems content to be on her own in the game room.

"You know the maid of honor usually has the privilege of throwing the bridal shower and bachelorette party," Stephanie mentioned as she skimmed over her pizza and went for her salad.

"Yes, I know," I replied since this is the third time she's mentioned it this week. "I never had a chance to celebrate those things when I had my shotgun wedding, so I'm looking forward to it. I just wish I had more time to plan."

"I know 4 months is cutting it close to plan a wedding but Brad and I can't wait to next year. We want to make it official ASAP. If you want, my cousin Rhonda can help with the planning. She's one of the bridesmaids."

"Okay," I would welcome the help. Kenny and I have been together since high school and I never had a chance to be a part of the normal wedding rituals. He was always overprotective and I couldn't get out much, especially if the threat of a good time with my friends was a possibility.

"Brad and I have an agreement, no strippers."

"Fine by me," my curiosity was piqued by the idea but at the same time as a mother of two I would feel ashamed in the presence of an exotic dancer. My mother would have a cow if she was still alive. The children played for a couple hours while Stephanie and I chatted. Still, we had to drag them away once we had our share of the day. Sherri called on the drive home but I have told Janise that I have dedicated their time for just them and made a note to call her later. Once we arrived back to the house, the kids went their separate ways to their rooms. So much for family time. I tried to get Sherri on the phone but she didn't answer. The kids are good about picking up after themselves but I haven't instilled the idea of chores like I should. Our home is modest and I don't mind taking the lead in the cleaning. Besides, I like things done a certain way and it is easier to just do it myself. As I grazed the carpets with the vacuum, I noticed the lights on my cellphone. I shut off the Kirby and inspected the missed calls. There were missed calls from Sherri and a number I didn't recognize. A voicemail from Rhonda instructed me to call her back.

I was surprised to hear from her so soon. I decided to call Rhonda first.

"I'm glad you got back with me," Rhonda spoke, "I have some ideas for the bachelorette party."

"Great, what did you have in mind?"

"Well a friend of mine knows the owner of the clubhouse on Blain, and we can get it at a 30% discount for the night."

"I know the place, it's a great location. I have a connection where I can get the decorations that fit the color scheme of Steph's wedding. And the food is already figured out. I just need some input on games. Should we bring gifts?"

"Of course! There is a baker on Elm street that can do an adult cake and you just leave the games and entertainment to me."

"Okay," I said hesitantly, "you know Stephanie and Brad agreed not to have exotic dancers."

"Well of course that's what she told Brad. It's up to you and me to make sure she enjoys her final night as a single woman."

"I don't know she sounded pretty certain."

"Trust me," Rhonda interrupted, "I know my cousin. Don't be such a prude. Leave the bachelorette party to me and you can work out the details of the bridal shower."

After my phone call with Rhonda I wasn't sure we would see eye to eye. As a newly single person I would love to explore some things I missed out on, but I don't want to go against Stephanie's wishes. And I know these things can get out of hand if not checked. Calling me a prude was a low blow. Just because I'm more mature than she seems to be doesn't mean I don't want to have a good time but everyone's definition of good seems to be different. Sherri would no doubt have an opinion on the matter so I tried her again with no response so I continued my cleaning. Just as I made my way to the family room with the vacuum I felt someone's presence behind me. Quickly I turned around and was relieved that it was Sherri.

"How did you get in?" I asked her.

"The door was unlocked. I didn't mean to scare you."

"That's okay. Have a seat; I know I could use one."

"Me too," she said as she flopped in the chair, "I love my nieces and nephew but it is hard work. I don't mean to sound selfish but I will be glad when my sister is done with her recovery. Never did I imagine being a full-time mom of three kids. I'm just not ready."

"It takes a lot of sacrifice, believe me I know. But when you focus on the love for your kids it's worth it. They're worth it."

"I love them, I do. It just happened so fast. I don't know what I would do without my parent's help. But I can't depend on them too much because they have their own health to worry about. Plus the added stress of Renee."

"You just have to focus on the positive," I replied in an effort to cheer her up. "Thankfully your sister is doing well and taking care of the kids is temporary. It's good that you were in a position to help her and your parents out."

"You're right," she conceded. But, I could tell it was still burdening her. "Anyway how are you doing with the divorce? You aren't going wild now that you are free I hope."

"No," I said trying not to roll my eyes. I love Sherri but she can sometimes be judgmental. Sometimes I think that she believes because we weren't all raised in a two family household like she was that we don't all have as good judgment as her.

"Just checking, you sounded a little hot for your computer guy and I wanted to be sure you let the ink dry before you latch on to the next batch of testosterone that you meet."

"My goodness, I make one joke and you go haywire. Since when were you elected relationship master," I argued.

"Low blow," she stated sounding hurt.

"I didn't mean it like that," I defended, "I just meant that I can navigate my single life. My mom may not be with me but I don't need a replacement, I want a friend."

"I know. It's just that any mention of a relationship makes me think of me and Tyler."

"It will take time but you will be able to move on," I comforted. I didn't really want to get into the Tyler thing again but I know it's bothering her. "Have you talked to him, for closure?"

"Not yet. I don't know if I should. I want to move on but as long as I keep thinking about him and her it holds me back. Maybe I need a vacation. You could come too! We can bring the kids."

"I would love to but I don't know if I would have the time since I'm planning this wedding and I have cut back my hours at work to spend time with the kids."

"Well a vacation will help you do that," she persisted.

"True. I'll have to see how it pans out."

"Fine, just let me know," she said as she got up to leave.

The next morning Kenny came by to pick up the kids. Even though I am at peace with the divorce, I still don't like being around him too much. Even though I emotionally broke things off with him some time ago, the idea of him sleeping with Renee and hiding a child still makes me feel some kind of way. Janise and Rod were already packed so I sent them out to meet Kenny while I rummaged the kitchen for breakfast. Since it's was a meal for one I settled on cereal.

"You didn't come speak," Kenny spoke startling me.

"Where are the kids?" I asked trying not to sound unsettled. I figured that he wouldn't be stupid enough to try anything but being around him still makes me tense.

"In the car. I just wanted to say hello. Just because we're divorced doesn't mean we can't be civil."

"I agree, but I really have a busy day, so…"

"Why are you so hard on me? I've been giving you space, I gave you your divorce, and I'm helping with the kids. What's the problem now?"

"The problem is that you think that means I owe you something. I don't," I said as I took my bowl to the other side of the counter. "I appreciate you reaching out to your kids but that is what you are supposed to do as their father. It isn't supposed to be some ploy to win favor with me."

"I can't take any more of this nonsense," he said forcefully, slamming his fist on the counter. He never took a step closer to me so I didn't panic. "You have to forgive me sometime. Every time you look at me I can see the hate in your eyes and I'm sick of it."

"Well that sounds like a personal problem," I said sternly. "I'm trying to forgive you but you aren't helping any. Now would be a good time to leave."

He stood for a minute begging with his eyes. Behind the pleas I could still see the anger simmering below and was thankful he finally turned to leave.

Chapter 12

Alexis

I had only been to Lex's studio once before but I felt comfortable entering the building. The security guard didn't even give me a second look so they must know who I am. As I followed the route Trina took the last time I realized I should have called first. I paused in the hallway after I got off the elevator and paced in front of the door. From the conversation inside I could tell that I found my brother and his friend J.O. Suddenly, I got nervous about what I came to discuss. Lex has never been exactly forthcoming about what he and my dad were involved with or how he solved my situation in college. Still, I took a deep breath to reassure myself and entered the room. Immediately both of their eyes were on me.
"Surprise," I said lightening the mood. This resulted in smiles from the two of them and Lex motioned for me to come over.
"Glad to see you," Lex said grabbing me in for a hug. I waved at J.O. and he did the same. "So, what's up?"
"We need to talk about the incident in college."
Lex and J.O. exchanged looks then Lex turned back to me.
"What about it? Is something wrong?"

"I don't know yet. Apparently, one of the cops, well former cop, has been following me."

Lex tried not to let his facial expression change, but I could tell that his jaws clenched a bit.

"How do you know?" he asked calmly. This piqued J.O.'s interest and he stood next to Lex.

"He tried to ask me out, we went on a few dates but something was off so I started avoiding him. Now that I'm seeing this reporter at work I found out that he was writing about the case that the cop was working on undercover with the SSM. They were going to infiltrate a drug deal going down with the SSM and the Rack Squad."

"So why is he following you?" Lex asked failing to hold in his anger this time.

"Somehow he knew I was dating Dante, and he hopes that I can lead him to Dante and Q. He thinks Q can prove that he wasn't dirty I guess."

Lex remained silent for a moment and regained his composure. J.O. spoke up, "well surely he knows by now that you aren't dealing with them."

"I still don't like it," Lex interrupted. "And you said this cat tried to date you? You aren't still talking to him are you?"

"No, but I was hoping to confront him and let him know that I'm not in touch with Dante anymore and tell him to back off."

"No!" Lex exclaimed forcefully.

"We could feed him info on Q to lure him away," J.O. suggested.

Lex looked at J.O. as if he was considering it.

"I don't like it. Just stay away from the cop and the reporter. You aren't involved in anything so you don't have to worry about anything."

"I'm worried about you," the words escaped before I realized it.

"Well don't. We will be fine. As far as I know those SSM boys are hiding out in Georgia and they don't have anything on us. The cop will have to move on eventually. And you know I have your back."

"So you didn't have anything to do with the drug deal," I pressed.

He seemed surprised that I was being so forward.

"No," he replied evenly.

"Did the break in at my apartment have anything to do with it?" I continued taking advantage of the moment.

"Some new members of the Rack Squad thought that they could get some doh by pushing old buttons, but I sqashed it. Like I said, you don't have anything to worry about. So find a new boyfriend and put all this behind you."

"Okay," I replied. My brother never shares information with me but I know he has never lied to me, so I believed him. But I don't know if I could keep my promise to stay out of it. With Isaiah following me around, he is dragging me in deeper. Lex placed his arm across my shoulders and led me out. "I mean it. Stay away from both of them; I don't trust them."

"Who put you in charge," I contested. Lex gave me a look telling me he meant business.

"Fine," I agreed reluctantly. "I will call you if anything else happens."

By the time I left Lex's studio I was late getting to WSJ. Since Glam burned down, I have been spending more time at my internship. Once Bridgette relocated me I decided to turn down the offer and focus on my journalism. It is a paid internship at the Journal, so I can get by for now. Alexis let me know that I can stay at her apartment as long as I need to. So far I have been good at avoiding Eugene. He hasn't pressed the issue. The only time we see each other is if it is work related. I stopped by Kina's office before I settled in.

"How you doing hon," I asked her. I sat in a chair across from her desk. Not the most comfortable seat but she doesn't have many visitors here.

"Hanging in there. I think I'm still in denial. Distractions are good. You up for a movie tonight."

"That will be great. I talked to Lex about Isaiah and Eugene."

"What did he say?"

"Not to worry and to stay away from them."

"Isaiah I can see, but why does he want you to stay clear of Eugene?"

"He doesn't trust him. He could be right. Who knows what the truth is? Anyway, I have a plan that will fit wonderfully into our dinner plans tonight."

"Uh oh," Kina said dropping her head to the side giving me the 'what are you up to now' glance.

"It's no big deal," I assured her, and myself, "I was thinking of calling Isaiah to meet me at the theater. You will be there to watch my back while I confront him with everything I found out."

"I don't know. Maybe your brother should be watching both our backs."

"No, he will just shut the whole thing down. He wants me to stay away from him. But I want to see if there is any other reason why he has been following me."

"I'm in, but if anything goes down, I'm calling Lex."

"Deal," I said. Then I gave her the fist bump to seal the deal and headed to my cubicle.

Most of my assignments are busy work but I'm hoping that the extra time I'm putting in here could lead to my opportunity for advancement. Heck, I'm here on a Saturday typing up notes of hair shows and notes from a lady who wanted a boob job and now has lop-sided breasts. Just as I was gathering my things to leave, I saw Eugene walking up the hall. I sat down quickly to get out of sight and thought of making a run for it in the opposite direction like I didn't see him. Before I finish calculating my plan, his tall frame was blocking my cubicle opening. He casually leaned on the wall. I wondered how such a flimsy cubicle divider could support his muscular build.

"Hey," was all I managed to get out. I stood up from the rolling chair and leaned against the desk for support. It seemed silly, but sitting with him hovering taller than me made me paranoid.

"You on your way out?" he asked.

"Yes, did you have something for me to do?"

"No, I just came to see you."

I didn't know what to say. I wasn't expecting him to be so direct. We have been playing the avoiding game since the altercation at the diner.

"How are you," he asked.

"Fine," I replied abruptly. Planting my feet, I stood taller giving off confidence I wasn't exactly feeling at the moment. I grabbed my purse to let him know I was planning to leave.

"Don't rush off. I want to apologize again for not being honest with you once I heard from former detective Harris."

"Okay," I replied coldly remembering my brother's advice. Yet, I felt as if I was being too hard on him. He may have been dishonest in the beginning but standing here he seems genuine. At least I want him to be. Still I couldn't risk it. I rearranged my purse on my shoulder and avoided eye contact.

"I won't hold you up." He straightened his posture as if he was about to leave. "By the way," he added, "I told Isaiah that you don't know anything, so hopefully he has moved on. I haven't heard from him since."

"Okay," I said calmly this time. He walked away and I started second guessing my plan that I concocted with Kina.

Sherri

My mother worked carelessly in the kitchen. Only an experienced parent can push away the daily stresses and still whip up a hearty meal for the family. Since she declined my help, I decided to go watch the football game with my father in the living room. The kids were playing video games in the den and I was relieved for the break. My father was engrossed in the game so I only received a nudge when I sat beside him. Watching the two teams back and forth I couldn't tell who was coming or going. Sports have never been my thing but I hate to be alone these days. Being alone means thinking about Tyler. This was a great pastime since he was never big on sports. But one of the teams was wearing red and it brought me back to the games that Alexis dragged me to in college. She is the biggest football fanatic I know. I remember times she sat on this couch with me just as engrossed in the game as my dad; probably more so. I do miss some things about Alexis but there are lines that were crossed. Tammy is still a part of my life but she has been on this family kick recently, and since everything blew up, things aren't the same. Being here in my parents' house remind me too much of the old days. Days I wish I could get back. Trying to keep Tyler off my mind is obviously not an option so I gave in. I had to call him. Back in my old room, I glanced again at the pictures on my mirror. I tore down the picture of Alexis, Kina, and

I. Then I grabbed the one of me with Tyler and Kina and ripped it to pieces. Then I ripped the pieces into pieces. I moved on to the picture of the four of us and ripped it apart too. This is where their act of betrayal has left our sisterhood. In pieces. I fought back tears and tried Tyler on the phone. He has been avoiding my calls but hopefully he can feel me willing him to answer.

"Yes," he answered the phone. That irritated me further. After all of our history, he answered the phone as if I'm reduced to being a mere annoyance; a telemarketer soliciting love that no longer exists. "Are you going to say anything?"

"Why," I finally responded, holding back my tears and what little remains of my dignity.

"There is no need to go through this."

"I need to know why. You at least owe me that."

"Fine," he replied forcefully. The anger shocked me. Here I thought I was the victim. "It has been over for a long time and don't pretend as if I haven't been trying to convince you of that."

"Every relationship has problems Tyler! I thought that we could work through things, but you went and laid up with one of my friends…"

"Exactly, you decided! You decided we can work through this. Just like you decided to kill our baby, and you decided that I would look at you the same afterwards just like you decide everything else."

"I can't believe you would bring that up," I shrieked. "I did that for you. All I heard when I told you I was pregnant was how we were both in school and how hard it would be for you to finish med school!"

"But you never heard me when I said we could make it work. Don't act as if you made this huge sacrifice for me, you snuck behind my back and had an abortion and then had the audacity to come back looking for gratitude as if you blessed me with a gift."

"I did us both a favor. If it was such a problem why are you just now making a big deal out of it? You are just trying to justify your lame excuses for doing my so called friend"

"I'm not looking for justification," Tyler responded more calmly. "You are right, what I did was wrong and I should have handled things better, and I'm sorry. I love you Sherri, I do. But, I'm not in love with you anymore. Because I love you I tried to make it work, tried to get over you overruling my decisions, tried to get over you choosing your friends over me, but I failed and I'm sorry. I wish things ended differently, if I could take it back I would. But the fact is this is the end."

I hung up the phone before he could finish his speech. The poison he spit kept ringing in my ears and I couldn't hold in all the hurt that it caused. I grabbed my pillow to my face and let out a scream that turned into an ugly cry. I couldn't let go, couldn't face what my life is now so I laid there crying. The pillow muffled my cries, but obviously not well enough. I heard footsteps approaching and I felt someone take a seat beside me on my bed. They laid their hand on my back and caressed me. There was no need to look up, because I knew who it was. It was the same caress that my mother gave me when I lay in this same bed crying. Dominique Wilson said that I could never be popular because I was too dark in front of Montrez Shaw, my second grade crush. In that moment I felt like that second grade girl, with the love of my mother reassuring me not to let the hate from others take my joy. This made me cry harder and I laid there in her arms.

Kina

My article was finished, my laptop off and back in the bag, but still I couldn't leave my desk. I stared off into space wondering how to go forward with my life. I could never take my life but I no longer know how to live it. Betraying my friend has ate away at me since I slept with Tyler and now I will forever have a reminder. A reminder that I want to love, need to love but still aches me to think about. I pulled out the sonogram that I received earlier this week and stared at what the doctor says is a baby. This ink blot now has to be my motivation. Tears escaped my eyes and I quickly wiped them away. Looking at the photo I know my relationship with Sherri is ruined. After hearing that she gave up her chance at motherhood I know she could never face me now that I'm carrying the seed of the love she lost. I can hardly face myself. Before I could lose myself in despair I heard my door opening and quickly put the sonogram away.

"You ready," Alexis asked.

"Yeah...Are you sure that you want to go through with this?"

"No," she confided. "But we have to know. I called Isaiah and he is meeting us at the theater."

"Okay," I agreed.

We were sitting at our seats, popcorn and sodas at hand. To the normal eye it would seem as if we are enjoying another romantic comedy. In reality I can't focus on the movie. We both searched the auditorium for Isaiah. I had only seen him in passing and the lighting wasn't helping me make a positive ID on anyone. I sat there anxiously eating my popcorn.

"Here he comes," Alexis whispered.

I froze in my seat. As he approached I sat up and nodded. I crossed my legs and placed my hands in my hoodie as if I were cool, but really I was getting a hold of my cell phone. Just in case. He whispered something to Alexis and she told me they were going outside to talk. I panicked. How could I do surveillance if they are outside? After they exited the theater auditorium I gathered our things and slowly lurked behind them. I've seen enough action movies to know that I needed to keep them in my line of sight but maintain a safe distance so I won't be spotted. At least I hoped that's what I was doing. I followed them to the parking lot and I waited behind a SUV. I could see them but I couldn't hear anything. I saw Alexis angrily moving her arms and then she calmed down to listen. Isaiah kept a safe distance so I didn't make a move. They were talking calmly now and I wanted to hear what they were saying. I couldn't get closer without being noticed. Just as I was attempting to dash behind the cars and come around the other side, Alexis came behind me and tapped me and I jumped up.

Before I can lash out about her sneaking up on me and almost giving me a heart attack, I noticed the ashen look on her face. "Rugga is here," she said.

Tammy

At first I enjoyed the break from the kids while they were with Kenny, now I'm starting to miss them. We may have to start alternating weekend visits. Since we have been spending more time together as a family, I have been looking forward to our family outings. Even Janise is opening up more. But I agreed to let them go with their father this weekend and now I'm at frozen yogurt shop with Stephanie's cousin Rhonda. We met here to go over plans for the bachelorette and bridal parties. I dismissed a call from Sherri and made a mental note to call her back later.

"This is Black Magic," she said showing me another photo of male exotic dancer.

"Really, I don't care who you choose. I'm still trying to wrap my head around the idea."

"Trust me. You are going to enjoy yourself. You're single now; it's time to live it up. Don't be such a killjoy."

I rolled my eyes. I have to get my girls back together. Stephanie is fun in doses but Rhonda may send me over the edge.

"Fine, if you think that this is what she will like," I said remembering her clear instructions of no strippers. The next hour I sat through her explaining lewd games I've never heard of. If I wasn't the maid of honor I would ditch the whole fiasco. At least I came up with some wonderful ideas for her bridal shower that I know Stephanie will love and her mother will be proud to attend. It is at a lovely private club called The Renaissance, and the décor is marvelous leaving little to be decorated.

At home, I grew restless in my empty house. Signs of my children lay everywhere. After a thorough cleaning there was still plenty of time left in the day. I tried calling Sherri back and there was no answer. With little to do, I decided to head into work and catch up on some things. Working part-time has been great for me and the kids but my managers have been complaining about this upcoming project. Since I have free time I figured I could get a head start on the work.

Being a Saturday the building was empty. I swiped my way to my office and let the security guard know I was here on the way. After a few hours of typing my bottom was getting restless in the chair. I knocked out the majority of some preliminary research and decided to take the rest home. I grabbed my laptop and the research I had so far and headed home. After I locked the door to my office I turned around and came face to face with someone I've never met before and dropped the files I was carrying.

"My apologies," the man stated. He reached down and grabbed my papers. "Here you go, Ms...."

"Tammy James," I flustered. I don't know if it was the shock of a tall, muscular, stranger in the building or his baritone voice that oozed authority that startled me. "And you are?"

"Jay Peterson," he offered. He extended his hand for a handshake.
"No, you're not," I countered. Peterson is the CEO of the company and his old pasty face is burnt in my memory and not in a good way. I took a step back and admired this mysterious intruder. He was casually dressed but he still evoked confidence and money. Maybe that was why I wasn't as frightened as I should be. His hair was long and up in a ponytail. His face was neatly decorated with a goatee and he looked more like a surfer than an executive.
"Jon Michael Peterson III. The old guy is my father."
I paused to reflect what he was suggesting. "I never knew Mr. Peterson had a son," I relaxed a little but I was still unsure if I should believe him.
"Yeah, my sister Kate is the golden child. But I come in handy now and then. I was just finishing up some work."
His story seemed plausible. If it wasn't, I was in no position to dispute it.
"Well, I'm headed out," I said extending my hand finally accepting the handshake, "Mr. Peterson."
"Call me Jay. I was on my way out too. Would you like to grab dinner? I know a great restaurant near here."
"No thank you," I shakily answered. Not only was I unsure of his identity, but if he was Jay Peterson I probably couldn't afford the restaurant he referred to.

"My treat," he insisted. "We have to take care of the employees who care enough to give up their Saturday to work in this place. I won't take no for an answer."

He started walking toward the door and motioned that I do the same. Reluctantly I followed unable to think of a viable excuse. As I followed him out I caught a whiff of his cologne and wondered if my lack of excuses was because I secretly wanted to go. My entire love life consisted of my now ex-husband. I knew it was too soon to start dating again, and I knew nothing good could come from seeing the boss' son but I couldn't turn away. Any inclination to beg off was swept away by the view of his Ashton Martin that sat in the front of the building. His driver loyally awaiting his return. My phone rang and I saw that it was Sherri calling back. This was my exit. Instead, I silenced the ringer and allowed the driver to help me into the car. Jay instructed the driver to head to The Villa and sat back in the seat next to me. His smile was charming but it was unsettling. The divorce may be final but I still feel out of my element and Sherri's voice was ringing in my head, 'let the ink dry first.' I broke eye contact and clasped my hands.

"You can relax," Jay spoke. "I may have his name but I don't have much authority here. I'm just the last resort when Kate is too busy or unable to come through."

"It's not that," I replied. I was concerned about the implications of dating the CEO's son, but the idea of dating was scarier.

"It's just a dinner," he assured me. "I only suggest the fun stuff on about a third date. This isn't officially a date, consider it a pre-date."

"Fun stuff?" I sat straighter in my seat trying to distance myself. For such a large car the space seemed awfully cramped.

He laughed. "Are you always this wound up?"

"I'm not wound," I stuttered. I thought about Rhonda calling me a prude. "You may have a well-known name, but I barely know you."

"Well, what do you want to know?" he asked. He sat back in the seat. He looked comfortable in his space.

"I don't know…Do you always take employees out to dinner?"

"Just the pretty ones."

A smile spread across my face. It has been a while since I've been on this side of a compliment.

Alexis

I dropped Kina off at the apartment and went to meet my brother, Lex. He told me to meet him at the studio. My brother is known for working late but I wondered if he wanted to meet at the studio to be out of earshot of his wife. I pulled into the parking lot and made my way through the building with more confidence this time. Inside the studio was Lex and J.O. and another guy that I'm sure I met before but couldn't recall his name.

"What's going on Lil Sis?" Lex asked. He sounded cheerful but I could tell he was anxious to hear what I had to say about my meeting with Isaiah. I was just glad that he wasn't fuming that I went behind his back and met with him anyway. Lex motioned for J.O. move so that I could have the seat next to him.

"Rugga is here. Isaiah told me," I cut to the chase.

"How does he know?" Lex asked.

"He saw him. According to Isaiah, that is why he was following me. He figured that if Rugga was here that I may know if Dante and his people were here too."

He glanced at J.O. who was casually leaning on the table near him.

"How does he know; has he seen him?" Lex asked.

"Yes. Do you think that's why they came after me, because he's back, feeling some kind of way about what happened."

"Maybe," Lex answered. He rubbed his chin and looked to his friend. "Smooth look into it," he addressed the guy that I couldn't place. Smooth grabbed his cellphone and left the room.

"You are still staying with your girl Kina, right?"

"Yes."

"Okay, head back and I will take care of it."

I was reluctant to leave. There were still questions that I wanted answers to. After I went against him once tonight, I figured it best not to press the issue right now.

Back at Kina's apartment I paced the floor thinking. Should I call Eugene? Should I see what else I could get out of Isaiah? Isaiah told me that he reached out to me after he spotted Rugga, and that was months ago. I wondered what had changed that made him comfortable enough to come back. Could Dante be back in town? I wish I could ask my brother what kind of 'agreement' he made with Rugga and why he had the audacity to come looking for a payout now.

"Would you sit down? You are making me nervous," Kina stated. She was in pajamas on the couch. I took a seat next to her and tried to focus on the reality show she was watching. Soon I was up pacing again.

"What is wrong with you?" she asked.

"You know what is wrong with me," I answered high pitched. I thought I was handling things well but once I got back to Kina's I started to unravel. "He's back. What if he comes after me again? What if I'm putting you in danger by being here?"

"Would you stop worrying. I had your back in college and I have it now. I'm sure Lex is on top of things. Too bad Sherri isn't here to nut check him again," she joked trying to lighten the mood.

The thought did make me laugh. After the deal with SSM went bad and Dante and Q went missing, Rugga snuck on campus and tried to grab me outside my dorm room. Sherri, Kina, and I were on our way back from a step show and we were headed to my room. I was lingering behind the two of them texting on my phone when he grabbed me. Thankfully Sherri turned around and kicked him in his family jewels and he dropped me and dropped to his knees. We ran to my room and called Lex.

"Well, I have my pepper spray and stun gun," I replied. I wasn't in the mood to talk about Sherri tonight. I smiled at Kina and continued my pace. I peeped out the blinds into the parking lot and noticed a black SUV in one of the parking spaces.

"Kina, come look," I exclaimed in a whisper. "Who do you think that is?" I asked once she was beside me.

"I don't know. Maybe you should call Lex, just in case."

She double checked the lock on the doors. I phoned my brother and he told me that he had Smooth and some of his other friends taking turns looking out for the apartment.

"Good, now you can stop pacing around my living room. You are wearing a track in my carpet," she joked.

"Girl, please, you were just as nervous as I was. 'hurry up and call Lex,'" I said mimicking her.

She threw a pillow from the sofa at me. I grabbed it and sat beside her on the chair.

"So what's the verdict on Eugene," I asked her.

"I think you are being too hard on him."

"He lied to me!"

"Withheld information," she defended.

I rolled my eyes at her, but she had a point. Even though he was dishonest, I would like to think it wasn't all a lie. With my past experiences I am already bordering on trust issues, and I know a relationship with Eugene would only be asking for trouble. Still there is so much I miss about him and I barely know him.

"You should call him," Kina advised as if she was reading my mind.

"I don't know...Besides, since when are you the dating expert," I said joking but from the look on her face I could tell she took it to heart. "I didn't mean it like that."

"I know. It's just that I've been thinking that my choices in men suck."

Her eyes started to water. I rested my arm around her and we lay back in the chair facing the television though neither of us was into the program anymore.

"This hormone stuff isn't going to have you crying all the time is it?" I joked.

Monday morning I rode with Kina to WSJ. We felt it would be safer to travel in pairs and cheaper on gas. My inbox tray on my desk was already full of notes waiting to be typed. By lunch I was more than half way through so I went to see if Kina was in her office. On the way I was stopped by Eugene.

"Can I see you in my office" he asked.

I followed him in then he shut the door behind us. In his defense there was a lot of sports paraphernalia in his office. Maybe he considered himself more a sports journalist than an investigative reporter.

"I can't believe you are a Steeler's fan," I said hoping to ease the tension.

"I can't believe you aren't," he countered then leaned on his desk. "Packers all day," I replied doing Rodger's 'double check.' "And the 49ers as long as they keep Kaepernick" I added, closing the space between us.

He rolled his eyes. "So how are you?" he finally asked.

"Okay," I lied. "You?"

"I miss you," he replied standing up. Then he closed the gap between us even further. I couldn't tell if the heat I felt radiated off of him or came from within me. As comfortable as I felt, I knew I had to take a step back.

"Really, you barely know me."

"I know that I miss you. We may not know each other that well but I would like to finish what we started."

"And what is that exactly?"

"Here we go with the labels again," he replied closing the gap again. "See, I would like to say a relationship but every time we make progress you fly away."

He brushed the fly-aways of my ponytail from my face and stared at me. Deep down I wanted him to kiss me and that is exactly why I moved away.

"Well if you hold a butterfly too tight you can damage its wings," I responded. I backed away and turned to leave the office. Even though I knew he was risky, I couldn't leave it at that so I turned back, "I'll see you around," I said then left, closing the door behind me.

Kina wasn't at her office so I went to grab a bite to eat. By the time I made it to the parking lot, I remembered I didn't drive. I decided to walk to the end of the block and grab a sub from the deli. On my way back I saw a face I recognized in the passenger seat of a car driving by. He had a scar above his eyebrow that I didn't remember, but it was definitely Rugga.

Chapter 13

Sherri

There was an incident at Derrick's daycare so I managed to get off early from work to pick him up. Any other time I would be grateful for the time off, but today was busy and I'm going to be slammed tomorrow. Besides, I relished the breaks from the kids these days, even if it did mean working more. Normally I would take the kids to my mom but she hasn't been feeling well, so I'm stuck with them again. Renee is out of the rehab facility and is staying at my apartment but she doesn't feel up to keeping the kids solo just yet. This is very convenient for her. It would seem that it would be easier to handle the kids why she is here, but my sister has become the complainer recently and seems depressed. So, it's as if I'm caring for four dependents. The upside is that Tammy's ex is in Derrick's life more and he spends time with him on the weekends. However, since Tommy is locked up the girls are home 24/7. I came in and dropped Derrick in my sister's lap then went in my room and shut the door. She could handle her own son for a few hours until the girls got home from school. I knew Tammy was at work but I sent her a text and told her to call me anyway. We made plans for me to visit her house and as soon as I picked the girls up from school I headed to Tammy's place.

"Hey stranger," I greeted her with a hug. I followed her into the kitchen where she was preparing dinner for the children.

"I know I've been so busy lately. How is everything?"

"Stressful, but we are doing better. How about you?" I took a seat on the bar stool next to her kitchen island.

"I'm good. Things have been crazy trying to plan all this wedding stuff."

"So, that's why you don't have time for a sister anymore," I joked.

"It's all love. You never got back to me; will you be able to attend the festivities?"

"I could use the break. It sounds like fun."

"So, I have some news..."

"Uh oh," I replied nervously.

"It's nothing bad. I went on a date recently with the boss' son," she said grinning.

"Wow," I replied not sure how I felt about the information.

"Well, it was just a dinner." She took a seat in the bar stool next to me.

"How did that happen."

"I was working Saturday, and I bumped into him. He invited me to dinner and that was that. He is really nice."

"Really."

"Really, is that all you have to say. Tell me how you really feel," she smiled.

Honestly, I didn't know what to feel. Men were the last thing on my mind since my break-up but why should that stop Tammy. "I don't know," I offered. "Will you be going out again?"

"I'm not sure. I haven't heard from him since the dinner. And I'm not sure if he is even interested in dating. Especially once he finds out I'm newly divorced with two children."

"Maybe, who knows, this may be the one," I surprised myself with the response. Tammy has been so encouraging to me and I didn't want to ruin her joy with what I truly felt. Which is that it's too soon to be dating and she doesn't have the time. Who knows how her crazy ex will react.

"I doubt that. Besides, like I said, I haven't heard from him since. What is new with you?"

"Nothing as long as I have the crumb snatchers invading my apartment. I'm literally living day to day trying not to pull my hair out. I'm still waiting on that vacation I talked about."

"I know, if only I had the time," she replied. She got up to stir the food. "You shouldn't let that stop you though, why not take your family?"

"I've thought about it. I know I said I wanted to take the kids originally, but now I've been thinking about a vacation with just the girls, or what's left of them."

"You know, a trip could be the bonding agent we need to get the crew back together."

The thought marinated. As much as I resented some of the things said, I could see a vacation with Sherri, Alexis and myself.

"Maybe."

Kina

The article I was working on kept me busy until well after 6. I finally gathered my things and went by Alexis' cubicle to see if she was ready but it was empty. I tried reaching her on her cell and there was no answer. I asked the lady next to her when she last saw Alexis and she couldn't remember. It was a long shot, but I checked with Eugene and he said he hadn't seen her since lunch and he thought she left early. I tried her cell phone again and left her a voicemail to call me. I wanted to believe she left early for the day, but I know my girl and she would have told me if she left. Still, I checked in with Lex to see if his people were still casing my place.

"I don't mean to worry you," I said, "but have you heard from Alexis recently?"

"Why, what's wrong?" he asked frantically. Immediately I realized I should have exhausted my options before alarming him.

"I'm sure it's no big deal, I lost track of her here at the Journal. I'll just try her cell again."

Once again she didn't answer. I didn't want to panic and I knew it was too early for a police report but with everything that's going on I was worried. I decided to take a walk outside to see if she was waiting in the car. There was no evidence that she had been waiting by the car, so I went back to check out her cubicle. Her

purse was gone but her laptop was still here. She normally takes it with her but I want to think that she just left in a hurry. That maybe she was waiting back at the apartment. I sped all the way home and ran into the apartment calling out her name. I tried her cellphone again with no answer. Now I was pacing the floor as she had been previously trying to assure myself that she was fine. But panic was starting to sink in. There was a knock on my door that made me jump. I slowly made my way to the door and saw Alexis' brother Lex through the peephole. I quickly turned the locks and let him in.
"Where is she," he asked.
"I don't know."
"You still haven't heard from her?"
"Not yet, maybe she…" he left before I could finish my guess. But it wasn't assuring either one of us. I heard him mumbling something to one of his friends and they took off in a jeep and Lex came back in.
"When did you last see her," he asked.
"At work, she rode with me this morning and when I got ready to leave I couldn't find her and no one has seen her since lunch." As I explained it to him I felt as if I let him down, tears started falling again.
"It's okay," he said. He placed his hand on my shoulder, to be a big brother he seemed uneasy around tears. "Did she leave a note or say anything?"

"No," I shrugged my shoulders. I wiped the steadily falling tears. "I'll try to call her again."

This time I left a more urgent message for her to call me back. Lex told me to let him know if I hear from her and then he left. It was getting harder to keep it together. She is the only family I have left really. She's the closest thing I have, thicker than blood. As much as I hated to make the phone call, I knew I had to.

"I don't know if you still want to hear from me but I have news," I said.

"What is it," Tammy asked.

"Alexis is missing," I replied and the tears came.

Alexis

My eyes slowly opened. I tried to place my surroundings. This was not Kina's apartment. The last thing I remembered was Rugga passing by in a car. I got off the cot to see where I was. I was in a small room with an empty closet and nothing else. It was dirty, there was no window and the door was locked. I paced the room again looking to see if I missed anything but there was only the cot. A dusty mattress without sheets on a rusty frame. The more I tried to relax the more I freaked out. I searched my pockets and they were empty. Once it sunk in that I was alone in this room without my purse, my phone, or my pepper spray I started to weep. I tried to contain it since I didn't know who or what was on the other side of the door. No longer able to stand I chose the dusty cot, my back to the wall, waiting. I rocked back in forth with no sense of time. I have no training for this. My plan was to keep calm and to wait for my brother. He knows what to do. The door burst open but it was not my brother on the other side.

Chapter 14

Tammy

"What do you mean she is missing? Are you sure?"
Kina was crying on my sofa. As much as I wanted to hate her I couldn't. We had a common goal right now. Find Alexis.
"Yes...I don't know. Ordinarily I would wait to panic but Rugga is back and this dirty cop, well I don't know if he's dirty, and she wasn't at work, she rode with me but she's gone..."
"Kina, calm down, you are rambling. What are you talking about?"
"The guy from college is here. The former cop working the case spotted him. And the cop was following Alexis. I don't know where she is, I don't know what to think."
Her head fell into her hands and she started crying louder. Instincts kicked in and I went to her.
"It's okay," was all I could say and hope it was the truth. "Would you like a drink?"
"No," she replied forcefully and then more calmly, "I mean, no thank you. I will be okay. I'm going to find her, I have to."
She stood to leave. The anger I had for her subsided and I couldn't let her leave, not like this.
"Maybe you should wait here, I'll call Sherri."

"Now I know I should leave. I'll call you if I hear from her." Then she was gone. She was right. Would Sherri care? I know she's hurting but she still has a heart and I know she loves Alexis. I dialed her number.

Kina

I couldn't just aimlessly wait. I had to do something. I headed back to WSJ to look for clues but came up short. I didn't know where else to go or what to do so I headed to Lex's house. I had only been there once before to see the baby so I drove a couple circles around the place before I finally found it. Trina answered the door.
"I don't know if you remember me, but I'm Alexis' friend Kina."
"I remember," she said, "come in."
I followed her inside towards a crying baby. It was Alexis' niece. She was much bigger than the last time I saw her. It is amazing how fast they grow in a couple of months.
"Is everything alright," she asked now holding Lexie.
"I don't know. I just came to see if Lex heard anything from his sister."
"I don't know. He rushed out of here without telling me anything. He was headed to his studio, you can try him there. Do you know what's going on?"Trina asked.
"That's what I'm trying to figure out," I answered. If Lex didn't tell her anything I wasn't sure if I was supposed to. She gave me directions to the studio and I sped off.
I arrived at the building and a security guard stopped me on the way in.
"I'm here to see Lex, it's about his sister."

He made a phone call then pointed me to the elevator.

"Third floor," he said then returned to his post.

As I got on the elevator I realized that I should have asked for more specific directions. Once I reached the third floor there was only one doorway. I approached it but before I could knock it was being opened. The man was easily six foot, clean shaven, bald, and looked shocked to see me.

"It's okay Smooth," I heard Lex say.

I wondered if he was named Smooth for the lack of hair or if that was coincidental.

"I'm sorry to barge in," I started.

"It's fine. I'm glad you came; I was just about to call. Have a seat." I obliged. I never spent much time with Lex but Alexis trusted him, and so I did too. The gangster looking company he kept I wasn't so sure about. There were three other men in the room and none of them looked happy.

"I don't want you to worry. I've heard from Alexis, and I will have her home soon."

"Well is she okay," I asked anxiously. His jaw tightened as if he was holding back emotion.

"She will be," he answered. He nodded to the direction of one of his guys and he began to speak.

"I'm J.O., when we found out that some members from Rack Squad were back in town we did some digging and found a couple of their trap houses."

"Alexis called earlier," Lex continued, "and they are holding her for ransom. I had Smooth check it out and I think I know where they are keeping her. You can wait back at your place and I will be in touch with you once we have her."

I nodded in affirmation. Smooth walked me back to the elevator and the ride home was a blur.

Alexis

There were two guys in the small room with me now. Rugga came earlier and had me call my brother. He demanded fifty thousand dollars for my return. Somehow I wondered if he would actually follow through. But I had to have faith, not in his worthless promise but in my brother. Rugga still spoke with his criminal charm that spooked more than comforted. I was relieved when he finally left. So far they hadn't tried anything but I didn't like the looks these two were giving me.

"Do you have to wait in here," I spoke up with newfound bravery, "it's not like I can go anywhere."

They exchanged looks and laughed then turned to leave closing the door behind them. Tears started to fall again despite my efforts to hold them back. I wiped my face and relaxed back on the cot. Anger built up inside me as I sat in this musty room and the sounds of their laughter made it back to me. Maybe kidnapping was a regular pastime for them. As I sat on the cot I tried to devise a plan that wouldn't get me killed or violated. I thought of lying about having to go to the bathroom, which was partially true, but it didn't fit in with the not getting violated plan. After some time the laughter stopped. I rose up to try the door again praying they forgot to lock it. They had. I slowly opened it and saw one of the men that were in this room was now sitting at a small glass table with mix-matched chairs. I tried to scan the rest of the place without being noticed. It looked to be a small house. I could only see the main room where the guy was sitting which was as dirty as this room. I heard a voice coming from the other end of the house and I shut the door. Now was not the time to be heroic. Maybe they would leave not realizing that the door to this room was unlocked. I paced the room but the stickiness of the floor was making me sick. I sat on the edge of the cot and waited for what seemed like an eternity.

Suddenly I heard a crashing noise and a lot of commotion. I jumped to my feet and there were sounds of men shouting and then gunshots. Afraid to run and afraid to stay, I chose the closet. I closed the closet door and there were more gunshots. I got low and covered my mouth. My natural response was to cry but I couldn't now. There was still a lot of crashing sounds and shouting so I stayed low, trying to remind myself to breathe. I couldn't recognize any voices; they all blurred together. Then I heard a crash at the door to this room. I went further into the closet but there wasn't much space to move. The door flew open and there was J.O. I ran to him and he dragged me out of the closet. I still heard commotion in the house. Afraid of what I would see I closed my eyes and let J.O. lead me out. I opened my eyes at the sound of running behind me and turned around to see my brother. He continued towards me and dragged me into his Expedition. J.O. sped off leaving the commotion behind us.

"You're all right," Lex said holding me near him. I wasn't sure if he said that to comfort me or himself.

"Thank you," I replied. I sat there under his loving arm in silence until we reached Kina's apartment.

"It's done now, okay? You don't have to worry about any of them anymore."

Lex kissed me on the forehead and I exited the jeep and promised to call him tomorrow. The adrenaline was wearing off and I could feel my legs unsteadily beneath me. I was filled with nervous energy as if I should sprint inside but couldn't find the strength. When I entered the apartment Kina jumped off the chair and met me halfway. The resolve to hold my tears that I had earlier weakened, and we stood there in each other's arms sharing tears.

Chapter 15

Sherri

My sister's journey to recovery was nearing its end. She finally moved in to her own place with her kids. As much of a headache as they were I will miss them in my own way. Renee had stopped by with the kids to pick up the last of the bags that were left at my place.

"Come back when you can't stay so long," I said playfully though I meant every word.

"Bye, Aunt Sherri," the kids said and I gave my sister a hug and closed the door behind them.

I took in a deep breath and plopped in front of the television. The television was on a children's program and I flipped the channel to Bravo to see which reality star was being featured today.

As I watched the catfight I thought maybe my life wasn't so bad. Tammy and I were getting along fine and I was planning on attending the bachelorette party for her friend Stephanie tomorrow. At first I planned on skipping the wedding activities because the kept reminding me that this was supposed to be the future for Tyler and I. But I took my mom's advice and I'm trying to move on. If I shut myself off I would be giving him power over me and I can't afford to give anything else of myself.

I headed to the kitchen and took out some leftovers my mom packed for me and relaxed in front of the television. This was my life now, television and work. It isn't as bad as it sounds. I made up with Alexis since she went missing but things are still awkward between us. She is sticking by the enemy and her evil spawn, so there is still tension between us. Tammy will forever be my girl and she has even dragged me to a few double dates with her executive boyfriend. Who would have picked me to be the single girl? Who would have thought that Judas was lurking in my circle and my friends would sympathize with the enemy? But these life lessons are shaping me for an even greater reward, I know it.

Kina

It is funny that I spent months on a diet kick and now I'm stuffing myself between the table and this chair, belly protruding over my lap. The diet is out the window and I'm eating whatever is in sight. Just as I was just about to dig in, my doorbell rang.

"You haven't been answering your phone," Tyler said, "I was worried."

"Usually people take the hint," I said irritated.

"Okay, you're mad; I will just blame it on the hormones."

"Whatever," I said hoping he would get to the point so that I could get back to my plate.

"I just wanted to say that the next time you go to the doctor, make sure they double check the heart. You know heart issues can be hereditary."

"Yeah, you might have mentioned it," I replied. Even though I was upset with Tyler and myself, I'm glad that he stood up to the plate as far as being a father. But right now he was irritating me.

"Okay I will leave you alone. By the way my mom said she can't make the baby shower but she will be dropping off a gift later."

"I figured that, your mom hates me."

"She doesn't hate you," he lied, "she hates the circumstances. Anyway, she knows how much my son means to me so…"

"Okay, fine," I said pushing him out of the doorway so that I could close the door. "I have to get ready, Alexis will be here soon."

Alexis was picking me up for the baby shower later but I was ready to get rid of Tyler now. I admit that the feelings are still there, and even though Sherri and I are no longer friends it still feels wrong to try to make a go of the relationship. At other times I feel as if I owe it to our son to try since Tyler is eager to, but one thing I've learned too late is to not rush things.

Getting ready for a baby shower was worse than getting ready for a date. Nothing fits and you have the nagging thought that all these people will be gawking at you and taking pictures. Some of my cousins and other relatives I barely see will be there, no doubt judging me. Just as I was considering ditching the whole thing Alexis walked in.
"You ready, 'mama', we're going to be late. And since I'm hosting this thing and you are the guest of honor, we have to get a move on."
"Do we have to," I whined and took a seat on my bed.
"Yes!"
"Okay, okay. It's just that I don't want all these people taking pictures of my belly. And I know that Tyler's uppity people will be less than pleasant, you know his mom isn't coming."

"Well I saw that one coming, but don't stress it. This day is about you and little man. Now get your big butt up and let's get a move on."

I laughed and took her extended hand.

"Let's go say hi to the haters," I joked.

"Forget 'em," she said, "thicker than blood."

We locked arms and headed out.

"Thicker than blood," I repeated.

Made in the USA
Lexington, KY
22 April 2015